Darius

Empire of the Sun

Dr. Alex Parsinia

Dedication

As I am reflecting and celebrating the publication of my second book, in the Achaemenid Dynasty series, and the production of the upcoming motion picture Cyrus: The Rise of Empire, I am giving thanks and gratitude to all people who have contributed to these projects, to our team, to my family and friends, my children (Bejon, Sarah, Christine) and my grandchildren, the so called Parsinia Tribe (Sabrina, Xerxes, Colin, Gabriella, Autumn, Eli, Sarah, Amber, and Willow), to my amazing mother Maryam who just turned 102, and to Mania who has given me joy and happiness. To my children and grandchildren, brother and sisters, family, and all the good souls around the world whose support, encouragement, inspiration, and love blessed my heart and sustained me in the years of living history.

Special Dedication

.......to the brave women and men of Iran fighting for their freedom and justice, this book is dedicated to you, Cyrus, Darius and Xeroxes are with you, their blood flows through your veins ....

Acknowledgements

Writing a book about the story of a man as great as King Darius requires great dedication, work ethic, and patience. None of that would have been possible without the constant provision, affection, and occasional rounds of healthy criticism from my team. The experience was both challenging and rewarding.

To my family and friends, thank you for being the people I could turn to during those nights when I just could not write anymore. It is because of your efforts and encouragement that I have a legacy to pass on and shine a light on the part of the Persian history where one did not exist before.

All of you have played a major role in getting this book completed. I know I might not have said it enough but thank you.

This project is based on 5 years of research, study, analysis, writing and editing. I would like to acknowledge the significant contributions of **Alan Bailey** who supported and guided this book as well as our movie project. He is the founder, CEO of Dynamic Media Group, Inc. based in Century City, California, which is a new media entertainment company with three operating divisions: Dynamic Media Network, the producer and distributor of Dynamic Media Network, the producer and distributor of high definition original TV content; Dynamic Media Music, the producer and distributor of original music content; and Dynamic Media Pictures, an independent motion picture and television production, finance and global distribution enterprise.

To **Adam Krentzman** who has had significant contributions and influence in converting our book into a movie. Adam Krentzman is one of the most well-respected executives in the motion picture business. As a longtime agent at CAA, Krentzman knows the entertainment industry landscape. CAA is the most prominent and esteemed motion picture, television, and music agency in the history of the entertainment industry.

To my dear friend and mentor who has been guiding me through this project **Armand Assante**. The award winning and one of the most elusive and yet prolific actors. Assante is a powerful actor who has successfully portrayed a wide range of intriguing characters from numerous ethnic backgrounds, both on screen and in the theater. He was sensational in **Gotti** as the head of the powerful Gambino crime family directed by Robert Harmon with Anthony

Quinn and William Forsythe. He made a sensational team with Antonio Banderas for the Cuban music spectacular The **Mambo Kings,** he was very impressive in the mob drama **Hoffa**, and once more he was on screen with Sylvester Stallone in the film adaptation of the futuristic comic book **Judge Dredd**, and Assante co-starred in the uneven Demi Moore film **Striptease**. Assante's acting talents remain in strong demand, and he has continued to stay busy on screen with recent appearances in **One Eyed King, Citizen Verdict, American Gangster** and **Two for the Money** with Al Pacino.

To the **Master Hojat Shakiba,** one of the leading contemporary Persian miniature painters. He studied art in the College of Fine Arts. He has held several exhibitions and shows around the globe. Some of his exhibitions were held in Museum of Contemporary Arts, Basel International at Switzerland, and Christies Gallery of London. His style is traditional yet with a spice of modern art. His art is a blend of the classic and the modern. His coloring and scenery are strikingly unique and original. Master Shakiba was gracious to allow us to include some of his paintings belonging to the Achaemenid Dynasty period.

To **Robert Jacques** who has been there when I really needed him and has a great compassion for our projects - Book & Movie. Thank you for your support.

To the entire group of supporters and contributors including **Jonathan Mitchell, Eugenia Gates, Nelson Alvarado, Robert** and **Andrea Kainz, Timmie Phillips** and **Josh Hepola**. Thank you for your support and enthusiasm. Thank you in believing in me, my story, and this new approach to epic historical writing and filmmaking.

To **Bill Gottlieb,** president of **Gorilla Pictures,** who graciously made his studio available to us and helped and assisted us in the production of our videos and trailers. Gottlieb has produced for some of the biggest names in Hollywood including Amazon Studios, NBC, HULU, Disney, and Warner Brothers.

To **Mania Minooyi,** who was patient with me as I spent long hours researching and writing and was my leading enthusiastic supporter and partner as we went to international film festivals and expos across the globe. Her inspiration and love have blessed my soul.

To **Parviz Barkhordar,** who is an author, editor, and radio personality and proficient in English, Persian, and Hebrew. He graciously took the task of translating my books from English to Hebrew. He and his wife **Vida Barkhordar** were enthusiastic supporter and assisted us in printing these books in Hebrew and distributing the book worldwide.

To **Monir Gheisari,** who translated this book into Persian and contributed to research as well as gathering contents for the manuscript. Ms. Gheisari holds a master's degree in international Law. She is the Managing Editor of Ranginkhat Publication. She is an author as well as translator and has translated more than 30 books.

To **Dr. Anahita Sardab,** a dear friend and confidant, who contributed significantly to this project by gathering contents and images from international sources. Dr. Sardab has a Ph.D. in International Law and Business Administration. She is the Editor of The International Law Journal and is involved in research and writing in the area of the Universal Declaration of Human Rights.

To **Dr. Al Khosravi,** who contributed significantly to the design of this book, cover pages as well as printing hard cover and soft cover books, posters, albums, and promotional items. His knowledge and passion for quality design and printing were immensely valuable.

I owe a debt of gratitude to my remarkable mother, **Mrs. Maryam Parsinia,** who just turned 102 and has been my guiding light throughout my life and to **Randi Parsinia, Sarah Parsinia, Christine Parsinia McIntyre, and Paul McIntyre** who have encouraged me throughout my life.

To my children (Bejon, Sarah and Christine) and grandchildren (Sabrina, Xerxes, Colin, Gabriela, Eli, Sarah and Amber), my brother and sisters, my family and all the good souls around the world whose support, encouragement, inspiration, and love blessed my heart and sustained me in the years of living history.

To the eccentric and internationally known artist **Davood Roostaei,** the founder of **"Cryptorealism"** Roostaei is by all definition, a classic case of a talented painter that seems to have found his path by illustrating his intentions and visions through multiple cryptic images. He is a painter of unusual intensity of expression.

To **Randi Parsinia** who patiently and enthusiastically edited my manuscript and contributed to the content and book design.

And finally, to many scholars, researchers, professors, and teachers who influenced my life to write in this genre and from whose work I gleaned much insight.

Professor Alex Parsinia Pepperdine University Malibu, California

About the Author

Dr. Alex Parsinia is a professor of Strategy and International Business. He was a Professor at Pepperdine University in Malibu and California State University in Los Angeles. He has taught courses in Strategy, Leadership, International Business, Managing Organizations, and Mergers and Acquisitions. He has a Bachelor of Science degree in Mechanical Engineering, Master of Business Administration, and Ph.D. in International Business.

Professor Parsinia is a prolific writer and researcher. He has published books and numerous professional articles in national and international journals. Dr. Parsinia has an extensive background in senior-level management, mergers and acquisitions, and more than 25 years of experience in the media, solar technology, manufacturing, and telecommunications industries.

Dr. Parsinia was the Chairman and CEO of Global Gateway Media in Los Angeles. He has been the CEO of Solar One Technology, Supertel Communications, JDS Services with revenues of over $500 million, Signet Paper Company, and Network Management. He was the President of TM TV based in Los Angeles, California. He has produced several documentaries and was the TV host for Global Crossing and Talk Money TV shows.

Dr. Alex Parsinia is the Producer of the Motion Picture Cyrus: The Rise of Empire. The movie is in the pre-production phase, and the story is based on this book. It is an epic historical movie based on the life and legacy of Cyrus the Great. A fast-paced drama of the life of Cyrus the Great that begins when he is kidnapped at birth because of prophecy and left to die in the wilderness. The beginnings of a heroic warrior destined to become the founder of an empire that would stretch from Egypt and

Europe to the Middle East and India. In the tradition of films like Braveheart, Gladiator, Ben-Hur, and the Ten Commandments, Cyrus the Great is an epic retelling of one of the most extraordinary men who ever lived.

Dr. Parsinia and his team of researchers are in the process of completing follow-up book related to the Achaemenid Empire - Xerxes: Clash of Empires. Which will be published by Blackstone Press.

*The Desire to know your soul will end all
other desires
~Rumi*

Preface

From the moment Darius participated in the plot to dethrone the fraud King Guamata, the cards of the Kingdom were set against him. He had saved Persia from an imposter, but, at every turn, the new king met with rebellions. He had people who were piling against him and armies who quelled his rule every time. However, that did not stop him from concurring land and becoming one of the most powerful king in the history of Persia.

Darius married Cyrus' daughter Atusa and converted to Zoroastrianism with the blessings of Ahura Mazda, he implemented a very effective and efficient strategy to administer the Persian Achaemenid Empire the largest empire the world had ever seen.

Darius, also known as Darius the Great, was the third Persian King of the Achaemenid Dynasty. His reign lasted 36 years, from 522 to 486 BCE. During this time, the Persian Empire reached its zenith as the first and only superpower of the ancient world. Darius was not a direct descendant of Cyrus the Great and became the king by a palace coup. After consolidating his power at home, Darius commenced vast military campaigns in Eastern Europe, Africa, India and initiated the start of the Greco-Persian wars. Darius is most renowned as being a great visionary and a genius as a strategist and administrator. He created the first formal legal system, monetary system, infrastructure, postal system, and he was an adherent of Zoroastrianism. After his death, the thronewas inherited by Xerxes, his son from his marriage with Atusa, the daughter of Cyrus the Great.

A Final Note

We live I n a time in which there are planned, concerted, and well-organized efforts by the present Iranian regime to eradicate the glorious ancient Persian heritage from our history books. We live in a time which Iranian history school-books coverage of Persian history starts on 636 AD, the date Arabs invaded Persia. Over the last 40 years, all accurate history books have been destroyed or removed from libraries, schools, and universities in Iran. Moreover, the present Iranian regime does not allow the publishers to republish these books. In the first invasion of Arabs, they leveled our libraries and burned our books, and now the present regime is completing the job of their barbarian ancestors.

As the result, our young generation in Iran and outside of Iran do not have an accurate knowledge about their history or identity. I know this by observing my children and grandchildren here in America. **Our youths in Exile are becoming fully westernized and our youths inside Iran are becoming fully brainwashed.** This is a huge tragedy, and it is our duty and responsibility to rectify this planned eradication. The young generation of Iranians have no clue about their rich 7,500 years old history. The Time is critical, and it is up to us to revive our Persian history and culture, or it shall forever be lost in abyss. The old saying: **You do not know your history; you lose your identity**. My goal is to contribute to the revival of the rich and glorious Persian history via educating the youth, inside Iran as well as outside, so they can regain and retain their self-identity in the world.

Contents

Page Left Blank Intentionally

Chapter 1: Cyrus' Last Battle

Below the soft hues of clouds parting the way for sunlight to shine through, the sight of the vast territory came into view. Through the fields of green came the dry sands that led up toward Massagetae. By many, they are regarded as a Scythian race. It was a city of Scythians built on a semi-nomadic life, with its people displaying remarkable fighting ability. There, through the land full of wagons and travelers, houses made of clay and columns standing amidst the city stood a palace rising high toward the sky.

Within the confines of the beautiful palace walls adorned with ornaments and gold sat Queen Tomyris. She was a Massagetaen leader ruling over her people. She was in her mid-forty and stunningly beautiful. Beside her sat her son, Prince Spargapises, the leader of the army. He was in his mid-twenty.

Cyrus The Great and Cassandane

Scythians were remarkable fighters who excelled in safeguarding their culture and protecting their territories. The Scythians were among the northern people characterized by red hair and blue-gray eyes. The Scythians were a group of north Iranian nomadic tribes, speaking an Old Iranian language (Scythian languages) who regularly invaded the northern territory of the Persian Empire. Queen Tomyris, a widow, was courageous and daring. She held her kingdom up to high standards, ensuring the safety of her people.

The method of fighting for both Massagetae and Scythians seemed similar but held subtle differences. The way of the Massagetae was fierce. They rode on horsebacks but also traveled on foot. Their cunning ability to wield an ax, both of gold or brass, was known far and wide. Their weapons were welded with gold, with intricate carvings on the surface.

Their customs, however, were quite different than the rest of the world. While they ensured one man had one wife, polyandry was accepted as well. One of the more remarkable features defining the Scythians was their treatment of their old.

From a young age, Queen Tomyris learned the culture of her people. She saw the old men being sacrificed, then their flesh being boiled and eaten amongst festivities. Meanwhile, the sicker ones were left to be mummified or buried. She ensured their traditions went on, but to do that, she had to keep her people secure and away from the rest of the world.

The Massageteans protected their honor and Queen. Queen Tomyris was the daughter of the Scythian tribe leader, King Spargapises. She inherited the kingdom after the death of her father, which went against the traditions of the kingdom at that time. It came as no surprise that the Queen herself had to fight to survive in a kingdom that tried its best to overthrow her.

She was married when her father was still alive to a proposal which she had chosen. Her heart was set on fulfilling her duties, but much more tense matters were presented to her.

Not only did Tomyris learn the tactics of battle, but she also excelled at horse riding. During the war with another Saka tribe, Tomyris' father called for aid from an ally, Kavad, who was the head of the Saka Tigrakhauda clan. However, instead of Kavad, Rustom, Kavad's favorite son, went to the encampment.

A competition had started at this time, and the prize was the hand of the leader's daughter, Tomyris. It was suggested that whosoever managed to catch Tomyris in the horse contest would be her husband. That was a challenge. She was amongst the best rider in the tribe, and only the best of the warriors would be able to overtake her. After an hour of riding, the sand blowing over with the hooves of the horses, Tomyris was finally caught by Rustom, thereby enabling him to marry her.

It wasn't long after Rustom and Queen Tomyris' marriage that Spargapises drew his last breath, leaving her with his inheritance and the position of the Queen. Tomyris then birthed her son, who she named Spargapises after her father. Soon, she watched as her husband, Rustom, went off to yet another battle, but this time, he would never return. She was the leader of a kingdom of growing influence and home to fierce worriers. However, the pressure of ruling on her own was still questioned by many.

Queen Tomyris

Her unmatched beauty had brought forward suitors, but they were all driven away. Queen Tomyris knew her heart lay within her kingdom and was not to be won over by a man. Regardless, she had a duty to her people.

There was no questioning her rule, and everyone who did learned why exactly she deserved the throne. However, she was oblivious to the turn of events that her life would take, settling her close into the path of history.

Queen Tomyris

As Queen Tomyris sat and held court with her advisors, a messenger made his way over to her. In his hand was a rolled-up sheet of papyrus tied with twine and a single rose within. She recognized the rose from her neighboring Achaemenid Empire. Immediately, she understood the nature of the message as well. Once she was informed that it was from Cyrus The Great, the King of the Persian Empire, she waved at the messenger to take his leave.

Cyrus the Great was known for his impressive military skills, bravery, benevolent leadership, and power. The vast Persian Empire was the largest and most powerful empire in the world. However, the warfare and unpredictable movements of the Scythian tribes were legendary. It was this and protection of his empire from the northern territories that had attracted Cyrus and made him aim for the expansion of his empire.

Cyrus' advancement first came in the sense of peace. An alliance was requested in the form of marital arrangements. Cyrus the Great, who had lost his beloved wife Cassandane to an illness years ago, had written to Queen Tomyris speaking of her unrivaled beauty. Later in the letter, he asked her to consider her marriage to him. However, she could read between the lines. Queen Tomyris understood that the proposal was a way to bring the kingdoms together and further expand Persian Empire. Enraged at the mere thought of it, Queen Tomyris tore the letter and sent Cyrus a strongly worded reply, warning him of any such advancements again.

After all her years of rule and learning the workings of her father's rulings, she knew the intent behind Cyrus' proposal. Queen Tomyris had an oath to her people, and no one else would take it away from her. Indeed, Queen Tomyris was exceptionally beautiful, but she had a sparkling intelligence that discerned every threat to her throne and prepared her to fight for it. Cyrus' name was well-known across the lands. The masses very much admired his exceptional military techniques and successes in battles against Media, Lydia, and Babylon.

Regardless, Queen Tomyris decided that she could not bring her people under his dominion. Although Cyrus accepted and even promoted different cultures, she knew it would eventually lead to the death of the Massagetaen ways. Queen Tomyris was determined to prevent the invasion of the Persian army into Massagetes territory. However, Persians started marching toward Araxes, which was an open declaration of hostile intent.

Prince Spargapises was the one who first learned of the advancements and later walked through the palace to consult his mother. He approached the door, carrying a silver helmet under his arm, the armor clinging to his chest. The pale white moonlight traveled into the dimly lit war room, and Queen Tomyris and her advisors glanced at the prince.

Prince Spargapises informed her of the Persian army's massive movements north and the construction of the bridges to cross the river. They decided that a warning had to be sent to Cyrus that he must leave the land or face the vicious brutality of the Massagetaen tribe. They sent a herald to Cyrus, hoping that he would change his mind about the war and withdraw from the Scythian territory.

The herald found Cyrus the Great amongst the soldiers, working furiously to complete three bridges across the River. Sweat beaded on his forehead, his face red underneath the bright sun as he carried logs along with the other soldiers. Cyrus did not notice the messenger until one of the soldiers pointed out a man wearing the Massagetaen colors and waiting beside a black horse.

"King of the Persia, cease to press this enterprise, for you cannot know if what you are doing will be of real advantage to you. Be content to rule in peace your own kingdom and bear to see us reign over the countries that are ours to govern. As, however, I know you will not choose to hearken to this counsel since there is nothing you less desire than peace and quietness, come now, if you are so mightily desirous of meeting the Massagetai in arms, leave your useless toil of bridge-making; let us retire three days' march from the riverbank, and do you come across with your soldiers; or, if you like better to give us battle on your side the stream, retire yourself an equal distance," the herald said to Cyrus. The intent was heard and understood, yet it was to be acted upon.

That night, the Persian chiefs were called, and all of them stood in a circle with Cyrus amongst them. Voices raised above the tent as the vote was laid out on whether they should let Queen Tomyris cross the stream and wage a battle upon Persian lands. While all of them agreed, there was one who stood on the sideline, opposing the threat that loomed over them.

Croesus was the ex-king of a Lydia who became a close confidant of Cyrus and had dedicated most of his life to giving Cyrus the best advice. The weight of his words outweighed those of others, and so, his opposition was very much valued.

When Cyrus turned to him, he said, "Oh! My king! I promised you long since that, as Zeus had given me into your hands, I would, to the best of my power, avert impending danger from your house. Alas! My own sufferings, by their very bitterness, have taught me to be keen-sighted of dangers." He paused for breath. His sharp green eyes fixed on Cyrus' face. He continued, "If you deem yourself an immortal and your army an army of immortals, my counsel will doubtless be thrown away upon you. But if you feel yourself to be a man, and a ruler of men, lay this first to heart that there is a wheel on which the affairs of men revolve and that its movement forbids the same man always to be fortunate."

Cyrus motioned for him to keep talking.

"Now, concerning the matter in hand, my judgment runs counter to the judgment of your other counselors. For if you agree to give the enemy entrance into the Persian territory, consider what risk is run. Lose the battle, and there with you, the whole kingdom is lost. For, assuredly, the Massagetai, if they win the fight, will not return to their homes but will push forward against the states of your empire. If you win the battle, then you win far less than if you were across the stream, where you might follow up your victory. For against your loss, if they defeat you on your own ground, must be set theirs in like case. Rout their army on the other side of the river, and you may push at once into the heart of their country. Moreover, it is intolerable for Cyrus, the son of Cambyses, to retire before and yield ground to a woman."

As his listeners remained silent, he added, "My counsel, therefore, is that we cross the stream, pushing forward as far as they shall fall back, then seek to get the better of them by stratagem. I am told they are unacquainted with the good things on which the Persians live and have never tasted the great delights of life. Let us then prepare a feast for them in our camp, let sheep be slaughtered without stint and the wine cups be filled full of noble liquor, and let all manner of dishes be prepared. Then leaving behind us our worst troops, let us fall back toward the river. Unless I very much mistake, when they see the good fare set out, they will forget all else and fall. Then it will remain for us to do our parts manfully."

When Cyrus heard the two plans and saw the contrast of it, he had a change of mind. He immediately chose Croesus' plan. The final decision was made, and the army marched forward.

There, underneath the blistering sun, marched the Persian army through the riverbank. The warmth of the water splashed as they moved. They went forward, not looking back. Soon, the sun overshadowed the soldiers, bringing the succession of the night. The sea of armored men laid out across the enemy land, resting underneath the starless sky.

The horses grew still as silence engulfed the land. There, amidst the serenity, lay Cyrus, looking up at the clear night sky. His tent cloth fluttered with the wind, but he ignored it. Slowly, the quiet night made way to the welcoming sounds of slumber.

In the darkness of the night, Cyrus had a vision. In it, he saw Hystaspes' eldest son, Darius, flying with wings upon his shoulders. When Cyrus opened his eyes again, the sun was glaring down on him, with the army getting up from the night's sleep.

The dream had cast the truth in Cyrus' mind, and the more he thought about it, the more he knew. The 20 year-old-boy, not yet in the battle, was plotting treason against Cyrus. Just as before, Cyrus was warned by the Gods above. While Hystaspes was sent back to Persia to watch over his son.

Cyrus' army moved forward. The day progressed, just as Croesus advised him. Cyrus had divided his army, with the strongest and the ablest men marching toward the river, while the rest stayed back at camp.

The word had reached Queen Tomyris and her son Prince Spargapises. Spargapises led the Massagetae army toward the oncoming attack. He had not realized that he was falling right into the trap, which was laid out for him. Cyrus had laid the camp with a few soldiers and filled the wagons with the most delicious Persian delicacies and wines. Once Prince Spargapises discovered the camp, his men slowly moved forward and, within the darkness of the night, attacked the camp, setting ablaze whatever they felt.

The joy of victory was soon enhanced by the discovery of the wines and food, and the men rejoiced by drinking the night away. The pastoral Scythians were not accustomed to drinking wine. Scythians used cannabis to smoke, make clothing, and in funerary rituals. However, they gorged themselves on the food and wine and fell into intoxication.

In their drunken state, the camp fell silent as the feast slowly died, and amidst the silence and snores, the Persian elite army, the immortals, appeared from the outside the camp. Soldiers attacked and killed the Scythian army slowly. Prince Spargapises was bound and taken prisoner. When the news reached Cyrus, he ordered that they should spare Prince Spargapises life and treat him with respect in captivity.

Queen Tomyris was a force to be reckoned with, and Spargapises knew of the shame that would befall him. Once the intoxication left his blood and he opened his eyes to a new day within the confines of the Persian army, shame had already crawled its way to him. Ashamed at the fate he had fallen into, he knew he could now not face his mother. He looked around at the tapestries covering the tent and the sword that lay close beside him. Slowly, he inched closer and positioned the blade toward himself. He lifted the sword, pointed it toward his chest, and pushed it forward in the blink of an eye. As crimson blood erupted from his chest, his eyes widened with pain. Darkness engulfed him soon, claiming his life.

The news of Spargapises' death reached Tomyris, and the loss of her son brought about great grief to the Queen. He had fallen at the hands of the Persians, and it was not something she would forgive. Once again, Tomyris sent a herald to Cyrus with a message to retreat and return to Persia, which Cyrus ignored. Queen Tomyris took hold of her entire army, all of them fierce and enraged, ready for blood. They marched to the battlefield. The plains of sand were covered with men and women of the Massagetae. The empress oversaw the war just as Persians marched forward. Cyrus sat in front of the line of the Persian army directing the battle.

Underneath the sun stood the two armies, facing each other, their weapons glistening in the light. It was not long before the horn was blown, and the battle cry rose amongst the lines of people.

Of all the combats in which the Persians had been engaged, this was the fiercest. At first, the archers shot their arrows at each other, and when their quivers were empty, the two armies clashed and fought hand-to-hand with daggers, lances, and axes. Both armies were fighting fiercely, neither choosing to give ground. Soon enough, red filled the grounds, and the sight of death eclipsed the once-serene lands. The valor of the men resonated across the skies.

The death of Cyrus in the battle with the Massagets, 530 BC.

Finally, the Massagetae got the upper hand, and the Persians were defeated with high casualties. Cyrus himself fell after receiving a poison arrow in the neck. Persians then took Cyrus' body to Pasargadae, Persia, where he was buried in a simple tomb.

Tomb of Cyrus The Great in Pasargadae, Persia

Chapter 2: Cambyses II

Dark clouds had settled over the vast Persian Empire at the loss of the great king. Within the confines of the large palace sat Cyrus' son, Cambyses II, adorned in white cloth with golden embroidery, a crown placed upon his head as he looked ahead toward the city.

"The king is dead," he began, spreading his arms toward his people as the guards stood close by keeping watch.

"I, Cambyses, son of Cyrus, the great king, king of the lands, king of Persia and Media, king of Babylon, king of the land of Sumer and Akad, king of Anshan, grandson of Cambyses, the great king will now rise," he said, using the names that Cyrus had given him before leaving for his campaign to Massagetae.

The Persian lords looked on, not knowing what they were getting ready to face. They were unaware of Cambyses' ways and wondered whether they could trust him to rule like his great father. The beginning of Cambyses' reign was relatively smooth. However, his judgments were full of controversies and brought about significant fortunes as well as misfortunes to the empire.

"He is no worthy successor of Cyrus the Great," some lords would often say, but their words never reached Cambyses' ears. It was the fear of his wrath that kept the public from making such comments openly.

The new king's inauguration took place in the New Year ceremony, where the city was full of activities. The death of Cyrus was a great loss to Persia, but the future of the Empire was soon dependent on his son's rule.

The king stepped out of his bath. He made his way toward his chamber, followed by the line of servants, each doing their duties to prepare Cambyses for the event. Apart from the servants, the palace was empty. Even Bardia, Cambyses' brother, was nowhere in sight. Once in his chamber, Cambyses looked out the window at the clear blue skies. Cold winds made their way into the chamber as he pushed aside the curtains.

"Your Highness?" One of the female servants called, grabbing his attention.

He turned toward her and saw her holding up Elamite clothing. He stepped back and allowed the servants to drape the clothing over him, first the trousers with leather strips, then the sheepskin coat with ornaments. Once he was ready, a few of his men walked into the chamber and helped adorn him with weaponry. The advisor sat quietly in the corner of the room, watching the new king getting ready for New Year's ceremony. "Your Highness, you must lay down your arms as you enter the temple," he said.

Without turning toward him, Cambyses' face twitched with a smile. "I am the king. I cannot risk putting my life in danger."

"Neither can you risk insulting the priests," the advisor replied. He was an old man who was well-known to the council and had been Cyrus's advisor as well. Cambyses said nothing in response. He simply looked at his reflection and then turned and walked out of the chamber.

The sun rose brightly up in the sky as the chilly winds blew past the hordes of people waiting to see their new king. Finally, past the dusty streets came the sound of hooves and the sight of the flags rising high in the sky, fluttering with the wind. People cheered as Cambyses came into view, riding toward the temple on his white horse. As soon as he reached the entrance, Cambyses stepped down from his horse. He placed a hand on the hilt of his sword, contemplating whether to remove his arms. His guards watched in patience and then proceeded forward as he did, carrying their weapons with them.

It was a simple mistake but a decision that cost him the blessing of the priests. The sheer disrespect was said to have caused the famine that later struck Babylon. People whispered amongst themselves that Ahuramazda did not approve of the new king, and so, he had sent his wrath in the form of a famine. Regardless, Cambyses accepted the crown and proceeded with his reign, ensuring that his people were well-cared for in whatever ways he could envision.

Cambyses II

Cambyses was still walking in his father's footsteps, trying to expand the Empire. His mind circled with the thoughts of Egypt, a conquest that his father had planned but had never managed to move forward with before his reign and life were cut short on the battlefield in Massagetae.

At this time, Cambyses appointed his brother, Bardia, at the position of the crown prince. He was aware of how his lack of heirs was a risk in the orderly succession of leadership of the empire. Based on the recommendations of his trusted advisors, he appointed Bardia in the position of being the successor in case Cambyses ever met with a tragic end. The thought of being succeeded by his brother was very much not his preference and often wakened him from his sleep at night.

While the beginning years of rein were rather smooth, Cambyses would still find himself lost in his thoughts, contending with the many issues that the vast Persian Empire confronted as the seasons passed. Finally, as the year dragged on and Cyrus' death was fading from the minds of his people, Cambyses decided that it was time for him to make his mark with the conquest of Egypt.

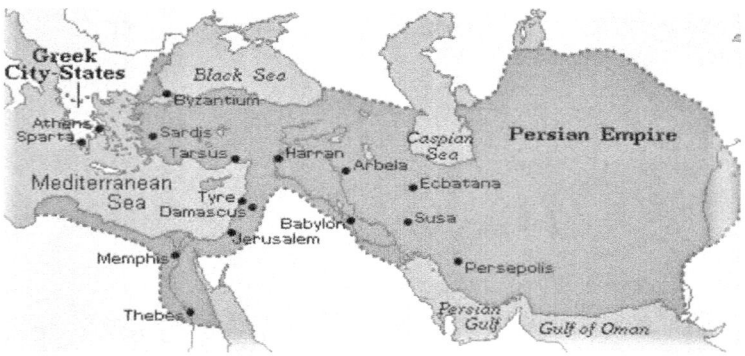

The winds of change had engulfed the vast Persian Empire, just as Cambyses prepared his army to head toward Egypt. However, while the invasion did settle in his mind, he knew he had to first tie any loose ends he had within the palace. His eyes, of course, were focused on his brother Bardia. He had finally made a decision about Bardia.

Before he left for his siege, Cambyses walked silently through the halls of the magnificent palace, his movements only tracked by the moonlight. There, within his chamber, sat Bardia. Hearing Cambyses out in the hallway, he stood up and walked out. He came face to face with his brother Cambyses.

Cambyses stood there, a cryptic smile on his face as he looked at Bardia. "Walk with me, brother, before I leave for Egypt," Cambyses said and turned toward the open area outside. He stopped briefly to pick up the glasses of wine he had poured into two goblets. He handed one of the goblets to Bardia, expecting swift and unquestioning obedience. He was, after all, Bardia's king. Their brotherhood was now buried under the weight of Cambyses' rightful kingship.

"The night is quite still tonight," Bardia commented. He took a deep breath as he walked out and felt the soft breeze caress his face.

Cambyses smiled and looked up at the moon. He had dismissed the palace guards, as he was accustomed to doing on some nights. It was a habit he had picked up a while ago, so it would not arouse suspicions when the time came for him to make his move.

"Yes, it is. It reminds me of how father used to go on his expeditions. Often, the nights would be just as still, as if saying that Ahuramazda was watching over him," Cambyses said and took a sip. He then turned to Bardia; his eyes flitted to the goblet in Bardia's hand before settling on his face.

Bardia smiled. The soft moonlight fell on the edges of his face, illuminating it. He was in his late twenties. His similarity with Cyrus was so evident in his smile, even in the darkness. Bardia took a sip and looked up.

"Sometimes I wonder how different it would be if he were here right now," he said, reminiscing about his dead father, who had raised him with so much love.

"Not so different. We would still be marching onto Egypt, but perhaps he would be accompanying us. Bardia, death is not always bad. He must be in peace now, with mother," Cambyses said. He turned his face toward his brother and saw a sad look in his eyes.

Confusion had now appeared on Bordia's face, which seemed to crumble like old parchment. Beads of sweat began to form on his forehead, and his head swam. It was obvious that delirium was claiming his senses. Slowly, the empty goblet began to slip from his hands. Before it could crash on the ground, however, Cambyses caught it.

"Don't fight it, brother," he said as he placed the goblet gently beside Bardia and placed his brother's head on his shoulders. He felt his brother gasp, struggling to breathe.

"Tell father I will make him proud," Cambyses said. Soon after, he felt his brother fall limp on top of him. Cambyses looked up at the sky and sighed, then stood up and dragged Bardia's body inside. He knew what he had to do next.

Bardia's death was not known amongst the Persian lords and people. Cambyses secretly buried him far from the palace and then informed his advisors that he had sent his brother to Ecbatana with some duties there. When Cambyses started to march toward Egypt, it was during the new reign of Pharaoh Amasis II. Cambyses had initially written to Amasis asking his daughter as a wife. The Pharaoh agreed and sent one of his daughters to Persepolis. However, when the girl arrived, she informed Cambyses that she was, in fact, the daughter of the previous Pharaoh, Pharaoh Apries.

Egyptian Princes

Insulted and enraged, Cambyses accused Pharaoh of sending him a fake wife and vowed revenge. Eventually, this miscalculation on the part of Egypt's ruler set the campaign of Egypt's invasion in motion. Cambyses gathered his men, and the entire army walked out of the city, their flags flickering in the breeze like captured birds.

The army marched across the Mediterranean coast and passed through the Sinai desert. It was the local Arabian chieftains who supplied Cambyses' army with fresh water and supplies.

Before the war started, Amasis II died, and his young son Psametik III was now the new Pherone of Egypt. He was young in his early twenties. His knowledge of warfare was quite limited. However, he did his best to prepare for war with the Persians.

Cambyses decided to send a Phoenician fleet along the Mediterranean coast with reinforcements and supplies. However, Psamtik heard of it and sent his admiral to stop it. Upon seeing the massive Persian fleet in the Mediterranean Sea, Psamtik's mission was soon shut down. It just so happened that the admiral switched sides, long before the battle could take place on the water. Psamtik now faced more challenges when his navy parted ways, siding with Persians instead.

Finally, after a long journey, Cambyses was able to reach the city of Pelusium near the mouth of the Nile river. Here, the Egyptian army awaited them, lines of men holding weapons that glistened underneath the sun. The Persian troops prepared themselves for battle, with Cambyses standing at the front. He looked over at his men and knew that they were ready for the battle.

"Today, we will secure these lands," Cambyses declared as he rode on, turning his head to look at his men lined up and ready for his orders. "Today, we will go from here victorious, and our victory will be remembered by Persians for years to come," he said, and the men listened quietly, directing respectful gazes at their king.

After the speech to his men, Cambyses turned to face the Egyptians. Slowly, he took his sword and pointed it to the front, signaling the beginning of the war. And so, on Egyptian lands, the battle commenced. Blood was spilled, and the grounds turned crimson. Once a large segment Egyptian army was destroyed, the victorious Persians made their way forward to lay siege to Memphis.

Memphis, too, fell. And thus, the army moved forward along the Nile, slowly taking over the lands and claiming them as part of the Persian Empire.

It was a victory of greatness, with the surrounding Libyan tribes and Greek states voluntarily submitting to Cambyses' rule. Finally, Cambyses made his way toward the capital, Sais. Cambyses was informed by his advisors that Egyptians held a deep emotional tie toward cats and considered cats as their beloved goddess.

Capitalizing on this information, he ordered the image of cats to be painted on his soldiers' shields. The Egyptian army, seeing its own beloved goddess on the shields of their enemy, was totally demoralized and fearing to injure the cats, surrendered its position and was totally defeated by the Persians. Psametik was taken prisoner. Cambyses spared his life. However, he tried to raise a revolt later and was executed.

The victory over Egypt was a huge triumph for Cambyses. Cambyses was walking in Cyrus' footsteps and emulating his father in expanding the

Persian Empire. Persian Empire now stretched across three continents: Asia, Europe, and Africa.

At the capital city of Sais, Cambyses was crowned in the temple of the goddess Neith and took the title of "king of Upper and Lower Egypt" based on traditional Egyptian custom.

Egypt

Cambyses' murdering of his brother Bardia did not settle well with him. He could not sleep well at night. He was known for his traits of madness which flared up regularly. His habits were very unlike most Persian kings. While he began his rule in Egypt and was trying to get accustomed to the Egyptian custom, his tendency toward insanity would appear. The death of Bardia occupied his thinking – his brother's last moments playing out repeatedly in his mind. He knew that he has killed his brother but was horrified to let anybody find out the truth.

On one sunny afternoon, much to the horror of Egyptians and Persians who waited and watched, Cambyses dug up the Pharaoh's grave while holding a lit torch in his hands. He then proceeded to throw the torch onto the corpse, watching the orange blaze and the black smoke rising from the grave. The stench of death filled up the surrounding areas. While the people watched in horror and slowly dispersing to their houses, Cambyses stood there, an ominous look on his face. He watched the crackling fire slowly die down and the ash blow away.

Egyptian Sacred Bull Apis

Just as the people had thought they had seen the worst of him, Cambyses proved, once again, that there was no predicting his behavior. In an Egyptian ceremony given by priests for his honor, Cambyses requested his guards to bring forward a newborn Apis calf, which was worshipped by the Egyptians and held religious importance. Cambyses, however, wanted to exert his power and instill fear in the newly conquered populace. He took the calf, and with his sword, slew it by piercing its thigh. He watched its blood form a river as it fell from the thrashing animal. Its lifeless body was then taken away and shown to the people who were totally horrified at the scene.

Cambyses in Memphis

Cambyses watched over his kingdom, ensuring that his grip remained strong and unopposed. However, Cambyses' authority was challenged when, much to his surprise, he received news from Persepolis about his brother Bardia claiming to be the legitimate king of Persia.

Cambyses sat in the throne room with his wife Roxanne, listening to a messenger who had come from Persia. Messenger's breath caught in his throat. He looked up at Cambyses and straightened his back.

"Your Highness, Bardia has declared himself the legitimate King of Persia in your absence."

The mention of Bardia startled Cambyses so that he sat up straight on his throne. The blood drained from his face, and he turned pale and cold. Roxanne took his hand.

"Bardia? Why would he do that? Does he mean to take the throne so openly?"

Cambyses looked at his wife with confusion on his face. "It cannot be Bardia," he said, immediately stood up, and grabbed his dagger.

"Prepare my horse," Cambyses ordered. He knew the rebellion rising against him could not be from his brother Bardia. How could it be? He had brought death to his brother himself before he left for Egypt.

"What is he saying?" Cambyses looked at the man.

"He has gathered an army saying that he is Bardia, the son of Cyrus, the brother of Cambyses II. He is declaring that he is the true king of Persia, Media, Lydia, and Babylon along with other provinces," the man informed.

Cambyses now began to pace. There was no choice but to come clean about the murder of Bardia. He informed Roxana, and his generals present in the room that his brother, long vanished from the palace, was dead. It was evident that an imposter had taken his place.

While some Persian generals did believe Cambyses, the rest were dejected about their king's approach. As the night transformed to daytime,

Cambyses gathered his thoughts and stepped out. He looked back at the Egyptian palace one last time and set out with his army toward Persepolis. He had to confront the man who was rising against him, claiming to be his dead brother.

However, what Cambyses did not know was that he was never going to meet the man who asserted to be his dead brother. Instead, as he rode on across the sandy plains, Cambyses' sword left its sheath, and in one swift motion, it stabbed his thigh in the same place Cambyses had pierced the Apis calf.

As the blood began to pour from his wound and the brightness of the day faded to black, Cambyses' soul slowly left his body. He faded into death shortly after, bleeding onto the sand that had once turned scarlet with Apis' blood. Cambyses met his end after eight years of reigning over the vast and powerful Persian Empire.

Roxanne

Chapter 3: Bardia, the Imposter

The sun shone brightly over the Persian Empire. As Cambyses' army marched out of the city, a wave of emptiness filled every nook and cranny of the city. The usual bustle had died away ever so slowly, leaving the people looking toward the empty palace. Its white walls traveled high up, and the chambers remained gracefully quiet.

However, from the silence that eclipsed the palace came the sound of rustling sheets and soft footsteps. A servant hurried towards the chamber, his bare feet thudding softly against the floor. He was holding a pitcher of water carefully in his hands, as though it were a baby.

Patizithes turned toward him from the mirror and flicked his fingers at the servant. Hurriedly, the servant ran over to him, poured the water in the goblet, and handed it to him.

"What news of Cambyses?" He asked as he turned to the mirror and looked at one of the soldiers standing by the door.

"He has left with his army. They plan to march towards Egypt," the servant said, his shoulders straight but his head bowed.

A smile slowly snuck onto Patizithes' face as he placed the goblet onto the servant's hands.

"Good," he said and turned toward the door, his robes swishing against the wind coming through the large windows. He walked out onto the veranda and looked at the luscious green trees. His eyes traveled across at the target placed in the distance. He snapped his fingers. Immediately, two servants ran to him with bows and arrows in their hands.

"Cambyses has left me as the custodian of the royal palace in his absence," he began and turned to glare at the two servants. Slowly, they backed away and ran into the palace. The soldier stepped up beside him and watched Patizithes take aim.

"What do you think of Cambyses?" He turned to the soldier, taking him by surprise.

The soldier looked at him, studying his expression. "His tyranny will surely earn him a place on the throne," he said.

"Tyrant, yes, but he is a bigger fool than he is a leader. His father, now that is a man, I can call a leader. He knew what needed to be done and the strategies to use...and the people to trust," Patizithes said finally, whispering his last words as if they were a secret.

The soldier looked at him in confusion.

"It shouldn't concern you, just that things are very much going to take a turn. I have a job for you, one that needs to be done in secret," he said, lifting his eyebrow at the soldier. "It's just a message," he reassured.

"Of course," the soldier said, taking a bow.

Patizithes turned his focus on the target once again. "I want you to fetch my brother, Gaumata, from Media. Tell him an urgent matter is at hand. Make sure no one is there," he said as he released the arrow, feeling the feathers on its end brush against his fingers.

"Yes, of course," the soldier said. He bowed and turned back.

Patizithes looked back at the target and smiled at the position of the arrow. "The winds of change are at hand," he whispered to himself and threw the bow at the ground. He turned around and walked inside.

***

Patizithes sat on the throne when the sound of hooves made its way into the great hall. Immediately, he stood up, walked toward the entrance, and smiled.

"Brother!" He laughed.

Guamata walked up to him for an embrace. One of the soldiers took the horse's leash and walked away while Guamata stood there and leaned close to Patizithes' ear.

"You said the matter was urgent. Is all well, brother?" Guamata asked.

Patizithes nodded. "Why don't you freshen up first? The journey is wearing you away," he replied and led Guamata inside. He snapped his fingers at one of the servants and ordered dinner to be prepared.

Guamata looked at Patizithes with an impressed smile. "Seems like you have quite a life here," he said and laughed.

"Indeed, now go and meet me in the dining hall," Patizithes said and watched one of the servants take his brother away.

The dining hall was greatly stretched out toward the back of the palace, and the table was adorned with fresh quail and fruits. The finest wine sat in the middle of the table with goblets placed in front of each seat. Guamata walked in with a smile on his face, which brightened at the sight of refreshments placed on the table.

"It has been days since I had proper food," he said, rubbing his hands.

He sat down and immediately dug into the poultry placed on his dish.

"Leave us," Patizithes commanded the servants.

They immediately bowed and rushed out the door. Guamata looked up from the food and then at his brother, his mouth full.

"Guamata, I have called you here for a reason," Patizithes began and took a seat next to his brother.

Guamata swallowed, slowly placed the remaining food down onto his plate, and looked up.

"Cambyses has left me in charge of the palace, but What if you and I were to take over the Persian empire? I have been in the palace for several months. There are things I have noticed. Cambyses has left his people. Who knows when he will return? You and I ... we have a glorious opportunity," he began, his eyes holding a glint of mischief.

Guamata looked at him and laughed. "Oh, Patizithes, you truly have gone mad," he said, beginning to take another bite.

But Patizithes grabbed the food from his hands. He turned Guamata toward him and looked into his eyes. It was clear that he meant business.

"Brother, Smerdis is dead."

The silence stretched across the great hall, Patizithes' whisper settling like the darkness that crept into every inch of the room. Guamata looked at him in disbelief then pointed to him. Patizithes shook his head.

"Not me. Cambyses didn't tell me, but he mentioned that Smerdis would not be around, which is why he was leaving me in charge. I knew his father. They both have a glint in their eye when they try to hide something. I tried to look around and found a gravesite not far from the palace. There was a body that wore the same ring I had seen Smerdis wear time and again. I had even asked him about it once," Patizithes said, whispering fiercely about his several encounters with Cyrus' family. He had been close with each of them over the years, and it was that which earned him this position.

Guamata sighed and shrugged his shoulders. "It seems impossible. Why would Cambyses kill his own brother?" He asked.

"Cambyses has always been known for his unruly nature and subsequent bouts of madness," Patizithes shrugged and popped a grape into his mouth. He leaned forward and smiled.

"Listen to me, Guamata. We have grown up looking at these princes and royalty and wondered what it would be like to rule. Now is our chance. You look just like Smerdis, so the people will not doubt it. We will rule these people the way we wish we were ruled and dine with riches beyond compare. You can own this palace and set all the wrongs right," Patizithes began excitedly and looked at his brother, hoping to find the same excitement.

Guamata looked into nothingness, his eyes glazing over with thoughts. A smile began to lurk on the sides of his mouth. Slowly, reality grasped him again, and he shook his head aggressively.

"No, this can't be. I'm just a Magian Priest. I know nothing about ruling an Empire," he said, holding his hands up as though in surrender.

"It's something you learn. Remember when we were young, how much our father would train us with the ways of the world. We were taught how to use swords and archery. We were trained for this moment!" Patizithes said. "Come on, brother. You know this is what you want," Patizithes continued and stood up, waving his arm around the room. "*This* is what you want!" He said and looked expectantly at Guamata.

Suddenly, a smile spread on Gautama's face, and he stood up.

"Alright. Let's do this," Guamata said.

Excitedly, Patizithes took up a goblet of wine and downed the drink.

"To the future," they cheered. The two brothers celebrated their plan in the night's darkness as the candles melted down into small stubs.

***

There was much to be done. However, Patizithes knew that the only thing that mattered now was the timing. The rising of a new king could not take place so soon after Cambyses' departure to Egypt.

Together, Patizithes and Guamata plotted how and when they would announce the news. It wasn't until years after Cambyses had left the Empire without a king that Guamata decided that the time was right to declare himself as the King of Persia.

Over the months, Patizithes prepared Guamata the fine details of royalty. The two brothers had prepared themselves for the backlash they might face and the challenges that might arise. However, when the time came to declare Guamata as King, they felt that the Empire was ready to accept the new king – most of them, at least.

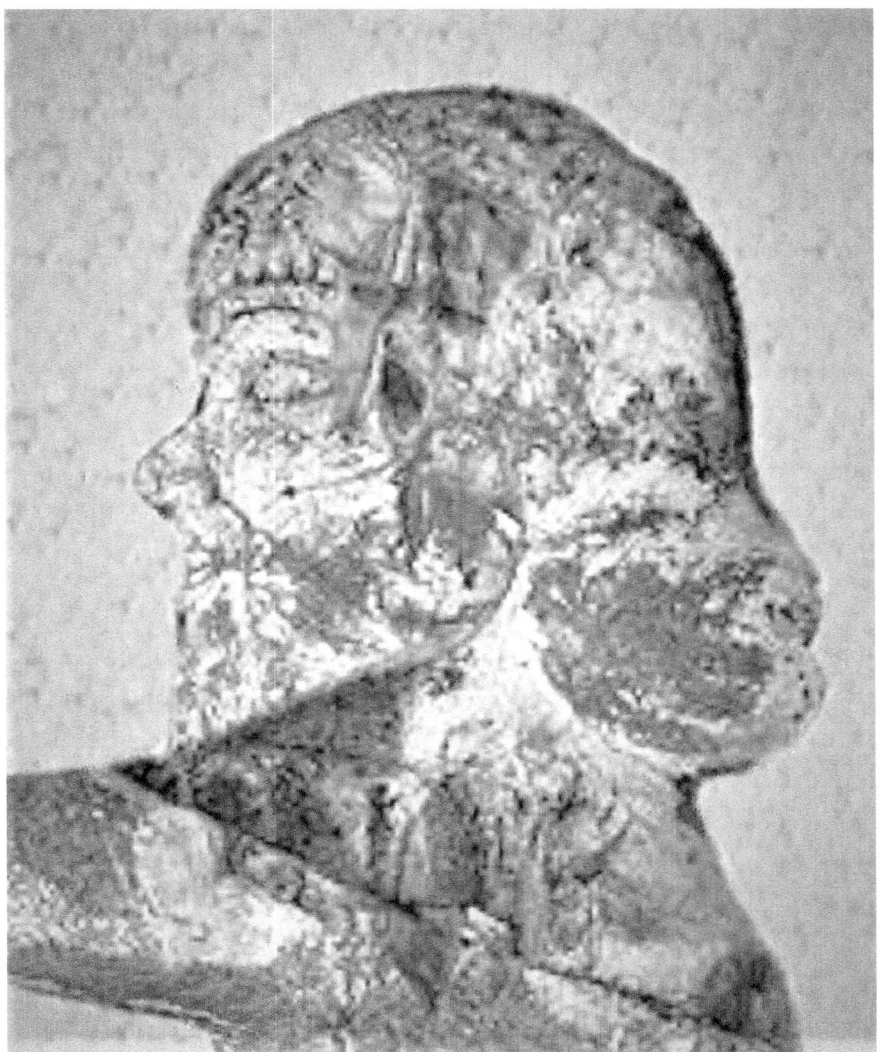

Carvings on Stone of Smerdis/Bardia at Mount Behistun

The Persians remained loyal to Cambyses, but Guamata offered them stability, continuity, and an offer of tax relief along with a three-year military draft and a promise of a king they could trust and believe in.

Before long, the day of inauguration came, and the Guamata was ready to capture the power of ruling the empire. He had marched forward in a rejoicing tone, claiming to be Bardia. He had only made his presence known amongst the people a few months and now stood in front of everyone to take the oath and officially earn the title of King of Persia.

When the sun rose over the kingdom welcoming its new ruler, the crowd gathered around the palace, looking over at the new King wearing a gold and white robe as he stood proudly at the altar looking over his people. He spread his arms out and smiled.

He was oblivious of who, amongst the people, had joined his inauguration. Guamata looked over at the crowd, focusing his attention on how he would now address his people. He cleared his throat, adjusted his stance, and began.

"I, Bardia, son of Cyrus, grandson of Cambyses, King of Persia, King of Babylon, King of Egypt, King of Summer and Akkad, King of the Four Corners of the world," Bardia began. He looked at his people, watching him in awe from a distance. They all stood transfixed in place as their eyes glimmered with newfound hope. Finally, Guamata finished the speech, sending peace to Cyrus, Cambyses, and kings before him. He turned around and disappeared inside as the crowd erupted in cheers and loud music.

Chapter 4: Gang of Seven

Guamata ruled the Empire as King of Persia and avoided most of the palace ceremonies where he had to be present and deliver speeches. However, there, within the gates of the Achaemenid palace, an uprising was beginning to take place. While he had most of the people believing that he was the true Bardia, some of the nobles knew that something was amiss.

Once Bardia was crowned king, the workings of the city changed. The palace was now filled with people unknown to the royal family. The old servants had all but vanished from their posts. It was a month after being crowned that Bardia returned into the city. He made his way through the crowd that stood around the palace, enjoying the festivities.

As the flower petals were thrown and music and celebrations went on, people swayed with the music. They tried to look up at the new king who had dismounted his horse. The guards were on high alert around him and paved a pathway through the people to enter the palace.

Darius looked up at him from the garden in the distance and took a sip of wine. He tilted his head to study him further as he passed by. He looked around at the people looking at their new king in awe. They all stood transfixed in place as their eyes glimmered with newfound hope.

Darius turned back to watch him disappear through the crowd of people until he felt a tap on his shoulders. When he turned, a little boy peered up at him and pointed toward a man standing at the entrance of a building; black robes adorned his body.

As soon as Darius looked at him, the man turned and walked inside the building. Darius reached into his pouch, handed the boy a coin, then looked once over at Smerdis. He sighed and walked over to the building, parting his way through the crowd. Even as the evening sun scorched the land, the entire city was out to watch the king enter the city. The strong smell of flowers mixed with sweat had now taken over the whole area.

Finally, Darius reached the building and walked inside only to find himself standing in front of Cyrus' grave. The large stone was carved with the name, and a flower lay atop it. Although the entire city rejoiced the crowning of a new king, there was an odd sense of belonging that vibrated around Cyrus' grave. Darius looked at the flower in confusion and then ran his hands over the gravestone.

"I placed the flowers there; you don't have to worry."

Darius jumped and looked back at the man who was now taking off the hood. His face was wrinkled, and silver hair streamed through his hair and beard.

"Otanes." Darius smiled and walked up to him, taking him in an embrace.

"We don't have time. The others have already gathered. You must come," he said and led the way.

"Where are we going?" Darius asked, but Otanes only quickened his pace through the alleyways, now and then looked around to see if he was being followed.

Darius kept up, feeling the shade of the alleys saving him from the blazing sun. Finally, they reached a large house with a dark brown gate. Otanes stood outside, took a deep breath, and rapped on the door, first knocking twice, then banged on it gently once, then knocked twice again. The door opened, and as soon as Darius entered, he saw that they were not alone.

There, in the large room, sat five noblemen that Darius had not seen before. He reluctantly walked inside, feeling the breeze coming in front of the door opening to the veranda. He went and took a seat by one of the leaner and friendlier-looking men, Hydarnes. He smiled and took Darius' hand.

"Hydarnes," he said.

"Darius, I've gathered the nobles here to discuss a matter of dire attention. You've met Hydarnes. This is Megabyzes, Intaphrenes, Gobryas, and Anspathines," Otanes said.

Darius nodded at each one of them. He recognized some of them from Cyrus' gatherings and councils. Otanes sat down on one of the chairs placed by the others and looked around, his expression grim.

"It's just as I suspected," Otanes began and poured himself some wine. He looked around the room and then settled his eyes straight at Darius.

"We have made a king of an imposter," he said. His words caused an eerie silence to spread through the room. Only the sounds of music and festivities made their way into the room now and then. The rest of the men slowly began to mutter in confusion, but Darius first spoke up. He looked at the old man sitting in front of him and stood up.

"What you're suspecting is profoundly serious. How are you sure that this is true?" He asked. He could not deny that he shared the same sentiments. It had been difficult for him to accept Bardia as well. He seemed so different than when he had met him last, a few years ago. However, the biggest thing he couldn't let go of was that Bardia had all but vanished from everyone's lives for years before coming forth and taking the king's title.

Darius and Bardia had often spent a large portion of their childhood together, and the mere thought of ruling the kingdom used to scare the man. Darius thought that his duties had finally caught up to him, along with his age. But now, as he heard the accusation being flung around the room, he couldn't deny that a part of him believed that it was, in fact, true.

Otanes was the Achaemenid judge and a nobleman of Persis. Darius knew he would not simply put forward an accusation without evidence. Otanes looked at him.

"When Cyrus was alive, there was a man, Guamata, who was brought to court. I was present in the room when Cyrus had commanded his ears to be cut off due to a grave reason. When Bardia rose from the ashes of what Cambyses had made of this Empire, I knew something was not right. He was familiar, he looked like Bardia, but his mannerisms were different. The only way I could tell if he was actually Bardia was to check if he had both his ears. Of course, I was incapable of doing it, which is why I have sent my daughter, Phaidyme, to confirm."

One of the noblemen stood up from his seat and began to pace.

"Then what of the true Bardia? If what you speak is the truth, then we must only think that Smerdis, Cyrus' son, has passed?" He said, his voice grave.

It was evident that no one had actually considered the death of Smerdis, yet it had to be true.

"It seems that this is not just a matter of treachery, but murder as well," he continued, scratching his beard.

"He must be punished!" Gobryas, a younger nobleman, stood up from his seat and began to draw his sword.

Darius immediately placed a gentle hand on his to stop him. "We cannot proceed without proof. It will be days yet until word about this reaches us. Guamata, as you say, is leaving the city tonight, which means your daughter may not be able to tell us anything until his return," Darius said, looking at him.

Otanes nodded.

"What would happen if he was, in fact, an imposter?" Darius asked something that the rest had been thinking.

"In that case, there is nothing else to do but to rid him from his position," one of the noblemen spoke up.

"And leave Persia without a ruler?" Another asked.

"Surely, Cambyses is still king. Once he hears of his kingdom being taken by an imposter, he will return to claim back his throne," Otanes said.

"It would still take months for Cambyses to return from Egypt. The journey is not so easy. We must take care of this quickly before Bardia learns that word of his truth has spread. No one shall speak of this meeting."

As Otanes concluded, the men fell into an agreement. However, there was much more to deal with at hand. As the men began to file out of the room, Darius stayed back and poured himself some wine. Otanes still sat on his chair and looked at him.

"How are you sure?" Darius asked, breaking the silence that was building up between the two. "Smerdis was always happy. He was never the man who wanted to rule, even when Cyrus would speak of it. I have seen Smerdis grow. And I was always welcome in the palace. Even after the mischiefs that Cambyses and Smerdis would do to keep Cyrus occupied with them, they would still welcome me. Now, Smerdis' speech has changed. His behavior and attitude toward people have changed. Most of all, he has forbidden anyone from entering the palace. We must speak to his advisor instead," he explained.

"It was the good old days, Darius. When Cyrus was alive, everything was different. No one would dare take a step against him. He tried so hard to make Cambyses like him, but he was too consumed by his own life," Otanes said, shaking his head.

Darius watched him and nodded.

"I have seen it too…the changes. I had not known before, but something did not seem right. Then one night, my horse bumped into Smerdis' outside the city, and immediately, his guards drew their swords. I tried to talk to Smerdis, but he hid away as though he didn't want to be seen. I did see him when he passed by, and he saw me, but it was as though he didn't recognize me. There was something different about him, about his eyes. I didn't think much about it until now. Now I know," he said.

Otanes shook his head grimly and stared out into the veranda. Darius stood up.

"Summon me as soon as you have a word. I will come as soon as I can."

Otanes nodded and stood up. "Be safe, my friend," he said.

Darius gave a quick nod as he walked out the door. The seven had already dispersed, and Otanes was left in the house alone. The meeting was a success, and the group was in agreement. It was yet to be clear how they would take care of Guamata.

***

The night was quiet, and the palace had grown still, except for the moans of Phaidyme echoing from the king's chamber. As she lay there beside Bardiya, her new husband, she breathed loudly and played with his hair.

Phaidyme

"You, my love, are the most beautiful woman I have ever laid my hands on," Guamata said as he laughed and kissed her once more.

"You only say that because I am your wife," Phaidyme smiled and turned her face to him, taking him in for a deeper kiss.

Guamata fell back into bed, put Phaidyme's hand on his bare chest, and looked outside.

"You know, sometimes I can't believe I'm here," he muttered as he looked out at the sky.

Phaidyme put her hand on his shoulder and moved closer. "But you were always destined to be King of Persia, were you not?" She said, confused.

Guamata shook his head and turned to kiss her lips. "No, my love. I meant beside you."

Phaidyme laughed and got up. She walked over and began pouring some wine in a goblet for him. She smiled as the bubbles formed on the surface and then dissolved into the drink.

Guamata took it, smiling gratefully, and downed it in one sip. Then he opened his arms to her. Phaidyme smiled at him, disrobed, and laid back into his arms, closing her eyes. Slowly, she moved her hands towards his hair.

Guamata took a deep breath and closed his eyes as his wife played with his locks. Slowly, she moved her hands towards his ears, recalling the favor her father had asked of her. Gautama's snores had begun, and she looked at his ears, moving her hands away from his head.

Slowly, Phaidyme pushed herself off the bed, careful not to awaken him. She dressed up quickly, put on her robe, and made for the gates of the palace. She snuck out from the servants' chambers and quickly made way toward her father's house, which was not so far from the palace.

Phaidyme knew her horse would attract too much attention, especially so late at night, so she chose to go on foot. She covered her face and kept looking back until finally, the house came into view. She held her scarf close around her face and knocked. After a few knocks, the door burst open.

"Phaidyme? What is it?" Oates asked, surprised, and opened the door wider for her. She walked inside and threw the scarf on the floor.

"Father. It's not Smerdis."

***

With the confirmation that he needed, Otanes knew he needed to act fast. Guamata had now begun to assemble his men to march west to Egypt. The group of seven knew that there would be no chance left for them to throw him from his position once that happened.

Otanes, once again, summoned the group of seven in urgency, knowing that there was no time to waste. However, they could not proceed without Darius, who was not in the city. Regardless, they assembled in the same house as before; only this time, there were six of them.

"Will Darius not be joining us?" Hydarnes asked as he took a seat.

"I have sent a letter to Darius for his urgent return. Hopefully, he will join us tonight," Otanes said. He looked over at the moon shining brightly overhead, lighting up the veranda. His eyes glistened with every lit candle, and he looked over at the faces, expectantly looking at him.

"Bardia, son of Cyrus, is dead," Otanes began, making the silence graver. He sat there and looked at the flickering flame.

"Guamata is now king, taking his place. Our suspicions were true," he continued.

"The people must know," one of the noblemen said as he leaned forward. However, they knew that the news would easily be considered treason, and the men's lives would be at stake.

"We would bear the same odds if we were to end his life," he said.

A familiar knock rang out in the silent room, and they all turned toward it.

"It's Darius," Otanes said as he stood up and opened the door.

Darius rushed inside, weary from the travel, and took off his cloak.

"I received the urgent letter," he said, sighing loudly.

Otanes nodded.

"So, it's true?" Darius confirmed. He looked over at the other noblemen and sat down.

"We must kill him. This needs to end. Already he is planning to march forward to Egypt. It will only be worse if we take action once he reaches there," he said.

"We must think of this carefully," Otanes said and sat down. His eyes flickered over to the moon as his mind reeled with thoughts. The silence only added more intensity to the impending doom that hovered over the dark horizon.

"I know what we must do," one of the noblemen stood up. The men discussed the plan in great detail until early into the morning and only realized it when the rooster's crows resonated outside.

Tired and drained, it was confirmed. They would carry out the plan once everyone was well-rested. The group of seven took a few more days to perfect their plot. The king had already set out with his army and was currently residing in the castle in Nisa. The group of seven packed their weapons and set out on their plan. As they galloped out of the city, they remained focused and true.

Hydarnes and Darius rode ahead while the other remained behind. They entered the city and took their positions by the castle as the others followed. Guamata had summoned guards around his keep, and so the five were responsible for fighting them off as Darius and Hydarnes headed inside. It was a night darker than most and the five looked over at the castle in the distance. Otanes looked over at the others and nodded.

"If today we die, we will die for the better of Persia," he said fiercely.

They nodded and took out their swords. Otanes looked to his left at the other two waiting in one of the corners and nodded. He hit his heels on the side of his horse, and the others followed behind him. Darius listened to the clink of sword and metal, and the sounds of screams erupting through the castle. He looked over at Hydarnes.

"It is time," he said, and the two got off their horses and rushed inside. They ran through the open gates, then through the fighting guards, occasionally lifting their swords to claim the lives of those that stood in their way. Blood spilled across the floors and on their armors, but they continued. Finally, they saw the chamber and burst through the door.

Guamata stood up, alarmed. "What is happening here?" He shouted.

"Guards!"

"They can't hear you, traitor!" Darius said, but before he could move forward, one of the guards ran through the door.

Hydarnes jumped in his way, lifting his sword to block the attack. "Go, Darius!" he yelled as he fought the guard.

Darius' eyes landed on Guamata. They locked their sights, not moving. In one swift movement, Darius ran to Guamata as he jumped to get his sword. Instead, Gaumata fell on the floor. He looked up just in time to see Darius looming over him.

"Please, don't kill me," he begged.

"You are definitely not fit to be king," Darius said and put his sword through Gautama's chest. He gasped in surprise and then looked at the sword. Blood began to pour from his mouth, and slowly, his head rolled on the floor. A thud caught Darius' attention, and he turned to see the guard lying lifeless on the floor with Hydarnes standing over him.

"It is over," Darius said and looked over at Guamata, whose eyes had lost all signs of life. The eerie silence of death clouded over the castle.

Chapter 5: Darius King of Persia

The news of the new king's death spread far and wide, and the conspirators hung up his head as a warning to those who dared to even think of committing such treason again. Patizithes met with a similar fate, for Otanes knew Bardia could not have reached such a position on his own.

The first few days after Bardia's assassination were spent cleansing the palace. Chaos had ensued, and all of his loyal subjects were given the option to either renounce the false king or meet with the blade. Of course, most of them chose to renounce Bardia, while the rest had their blood covering the sands of Persia.

However, Persia was now left without a king. The Gang of Seven had to come to a decision quickly before the entire empire was doomed to the tyranny of outsiders. Once the chaos settled down, and the quiet once again took over the empire, the conspirators met again to come to a decision about the rule. With Bardia's head still adorning the palace walls, the sounds of hooves resounded over the horizon. The seven rode fast toward their destination.

Darius looked over at the palace that was once so alive with signs of life. He gave the reins of his horse to one of the men standing guard and followed the rest of the seven into the great hall. They seated themselves in the dining hall where Patizithes and his brother once sat to conspire against Cambyses. Now the eerie emptiness echoed in the dreary space.

"What must be done of Persia? We need a ruler, and after the death of Cambyses, it seems there is no one worthy enough to take hold of that position," Anspathines began. He walked over to one of the chairs and sat down.

"I believe that the successor must be one of us," Hydarnes cautiously ventured. He looked around to see everyone studying him.

Anspathines scratched his beard as he thought about it. The speeches had begun, with each one getting their fair share of insights and ideas shared. Their voices rang up from above the table and into the halls outside, echoing in the vacant palace. The ghosts of the past kings watched over the decisions being hurled about the future of the empire.

"I say that the management of public affairs should be entrusted to the whole nation," Otanes finally spoke, after quietly witnessing the seven share their ideas.

"You mean to say a democracy?" Gobryas confirmed.

Otanes nodded and stood up. "I believe it is advisable not to have a single man to rule over us. Over the past rules, it is seen that the rule of one is neither good nor pleasant. Have you forgotten the length of Cambyses' tyranny as well as the greed that accompanied the Magi?" He paused, feeling the gaze of every man in the hall on his face. He continued, "You all have only just experienced it yourselves. How then can we claim that a monarchy would be a better scheme when it allows a man to do as he likes without being answerable? It is this license which brings about such terrible thoughts and darkness to take over the hearts of some of the worthiest men."

From the corner of his eye, Otanes noticed some men nodding their assent. He forged ahead, "Once you give a man such a person, it will immediately fill him with pride and envy – two of the most common wickedness which undoubtedly arises in men. Both of these together lead to incomprehensible violence, and only the weak suffer the brunt of such darkness of the mind. It, indeed, is true that the kings have possession of everything they desire, and they must be void of envy. But it is clearly visible in how they treat their people."

Otanes then looked at each of the men, his eyes stopping at Darius. He looked Darius straight in the eyes. It was as though the two exchanged unspoken but eloquent words. He then looked away, fixing his eyes on others.

"Often, kings are jealous of the subjects who are most virtuous and end up wishing for their deaths. On the other hand, they take delight in the meanest and only listen to tales spoken by slanderers. A king is also beyond all other men inconsistent with himself. He needs profound respect and does not pay heed to moderation. But if you give him profound respect, then he is, once again, offended for how you fawn over him."

The men watched Otanes, silently soaking up his words borne of wisdom and years of experience.

Otanes held up a hand and said, "But of all the things a king does, the worst is that he sets aside the laws of the land, then he sends men to their deaths without trial and submits women to violence."

The men could not help but agree.

"If we choose democracy," Otanes asserted, "It will be fair and free from the outrages otherwise committed by a king. Places will be given by the lot, and the magistrate will be answerable for his actions. The measures will lie with commonality. So tell me, brothers, what you say about doing away with monarchy, and give people the power instead?"

A hush fell over the room as Otanes looked around. Before anyone else could speak, Megabyzus cleared his throat and gained the attention of everyone around.

"Otanes is trying to persuade you all to turn away from the years of monarchy in this land, and I would say that I have to concur. I believe that calling people to power may not serve well for the empire. For there is nothing so void of understanding."

Megabyzus looked at Otanes, who nodded at him to continue speaking. Megabyzus said, "There is no sense in men who form a mob to seek an escape from the wantonness of a tyrant. While a tyrant has an understanding of his proceedings, a mob is often devoid of such knowledge. A mob will have no understanding of rightness and the fitting policies for the benefit of an Empire. They will rush wildly in a stream of fury and confuse even those who seek reason."

Drawing a deep breath, Megabyzus insisted, "I say, we let the enemies of the Persia be ruled by democracies. We will, however, choose from the citizens, a certain number of the worthiest and put the Empire in their hands."

Looks of confusion spread around the room. The silence resounded with an unspoken question. What did Megabyzus mean?

The man did not delay answering. "We, ourselves, shall be among the governors, but the power shall be endowed on the best of men and whose counsels shall bring the state to success."

As Megabyzus quieted down, a string of murmurs rose. Each nobleman considered the words from Megabyzus, knowing that he was, to some extent, right. The creaking of the chair made them all turn to Darius, who had now risen from his seat, deep in thought.

"I agree with Megabyzus; democracy is not the right option. But oligarchy may not be a wise decision. Let us take these three forms of government – oligarchy, monarchy, and democracy. I believe that monarchy is the one that stands above the two. Will a government truly be better than one man in the entire state? The counsels of such a man are like himself, and so he governs the mass of the people to their heart's content. At the same time, he is able to keep the measures against the transgressors secret than in other states."

Darius cleared his throat before continuing, "In oligarchies, men live for the commonwealth, and enmities are bound to arise amongst them. Each of them will wish to rise above the other and be the leader to carry out his policies. The quarrels lead to open strife and finally, bloodshed in which case, monarchy shall prevail."

Darius glanced at every face in the room to check whether they were following. Then he added, "In a democracy, we would not be able to remove malpractices. However, it is seen that these would not lead to enmities but to close friendships. Those friendships would be formed by the ones engaged in them and be together for their villainies. It will carry on until the time a man would stand as the champion of the commonalty while putting away the evil-doers. Immediately, this man will be admired for such a great service and appointed as a king. Indeed, it is seen that, once again, monarchy is the best government."

Silence descended in the hall once more. Darius opened both his hands and stretched them, palm out, where his companions sat, listening and watching him.

"I ask you all, was it the freedom we received that we enjoyed? What government will be able to give us that freedom? One man, Cyrus The Great, gave us our freedom, and I say that we continue to keep that rule. We must also not change the laws of our forefathers when they work fairly, for to do so is not well."

Darius took a moment for his words to settle. Quietly, he made his way back to his chair and sat down. Intaphrenes turned to the rest of the people sitting in the council and discussed the matter. Darius turned to Otanes, who turned to him and nodded.

"What say you, seven? What must be made of the governments?" Otanes finally asked as the murmurs subsided.

They all turned to the people on the table, the silence stretching out in front of them.

"We vote in favor of Darius. Indeed, a monarchy will be the best way forward for the empire," one of the noblemen said. His eyes traveled to the redness spreading across Otanes' face.

"All of you?" He asked and was returned by an affirming nod. Otanes sighed and calmed himself, gently rubbing his hand. Slowly, he rose from his seat once again and walked up to them.

"My brother conspirators. As Hydarnes had said, the new ruler of this great Empire will be from amongst ourselves. Whether we choose it or let the people do so, the new ruler will be someone from this room. I, for one, do not have the mind to rule or to be ruled. I will respectfully set myself away, but on one condition." He put his hands together and looked at all of those present in the room.

"What is that?" Darius asked, making Otanes turn to him.

"None of you shall claim to exercise rule over me or my seed forever," he said as a hush fell over the room.

Each of the noblemen looked at him and then each other. Slowly, they all nodded in agreement.

"So be it as you may," Intaphrenes said.

Otanes nodded and stood aside.

"As for the rest, how will we decide who becomes the king?" Darius asked.

"I know a way. It was practiced by some people when I was a child, and the elders would come to a disagreement and could not choose between two people," Gobryas said.

"There would be a ceremony of sorts in those days, and the elders would take their horses out of the village. The first horse to neigh with the morning light would win."

The noblemen all turned to each other and nodded.

"It is settled then. We leave before the rooster crows," Darius said, smiling.

Intaphrenes nodded and turned to Otanes, who sat at the end of the table.

"I believe that, while Otanes has chosen to bow out of the competition, it is necessary that he, too, receives some reward. After all, he is the one who brought us all together and told us of Bardia, the imposter," he said and smiled.

Otanes began to protest, but Intaphrenes held up a hand.

"I say that, if any of us receives the monarchy, then Otanes, his children, and the generations after them should receive, as a mark of special honor, a Median Robe," Anspathines began, and then Intaphrenes continued.

"Along with all other gifts as are accounted the most honorable in Persia."

A round of agreements ensued as Otanes sat there humbly, looking at each of the conspirators.

"I thank you all. Together, we will restore Persia to its glory. Overthrowing Bardia was a great achievement indeed, and I am proud to have stood beside each of you in doing so," Otanes said.

Intaphrenes walked over to him and placed a hand on his shoulder. He looked deep into Otanes' eyes and nodded. "It would not have been possible without your humble guidance, brother," he smiled.

"Let us rejoice in the achievement," He said, and the men all cheered.

They spent that night discussing the privileges that each of them would receive. After a lot of discussions, it was decided that they would all, including Otanes, be free to enter the palace unannounced. This was unless the king was in the company of one of his wives. The person who would be claimed as the king would be bound to marry into only the conspirators' families.

Once it was accepted, the men dispersed to their homes to prepare themselves for the next morning.

As the day died away, Darius sat up all night looking up at the stars. He sighed as he watched the moon shine bright in the sky, its white hues of light eclipsing the surroundings. Darius watched the clouds pass through, moving as the winds whipped across his face.

"I have never even dreamed of being a king, but it already feels as though I am," Darius plucked a blade of grass and twirled it in his hand.

"God, the decision is yours, but have my horse be on my side. Grant me the position of the King of Persia that has suddenly seemed so true," he whispered and then turned back to the sound of footsteps. He saw a young man walk up toward him with his hands clumsily hanging on either side. Even in the darkness, there was a flicker of mischief in his eyes.

"Master?" He asked and stood up, clapping the dust off his hands and clothes.

"Yes, Oibares," Darius said and smiled.

Oibares was a sharp-witted knave who Darius had called for immediately after the meeting dispersed.

"Oibares, this is a matter of grave importance. You see, a king is yet to be chosen, and I need your help with it," he began.

A smile formed on Oibares' face. He looked around and then intently leaned in.

"Yes, master."

"We will mount our horses and ride out of the city. The horse that neighs at first sight of dawn will be crowned King of Persia. If you have any cleverness, then I believe that you can contrive a plan for the prize to be ours and ours alone," Darius said.

"Of course, master. If this test determines the fate of the empire, then you should have no fear. I have a trick up my sleeve which will definitely not fail," Oibares said mischievously.

Darius smiled, put a hand on his shoulder, and leaned closer to him.

"If you have such a plan, then waste no time. The matter will not be delayed because the trial shall take place tomorrow," Darius said.

Darius – A Painting by the Master Shakiba

"Yes, master," Oibares said and then turned around.

Darius watched as he ran out of his sight, then headed home. A knock on the door grabbed Darius' attention. He stood up and got dressed. Then he headed down the stairs. As he opened the door, Hydarnes stood there with a smile on his face, holding his horse's reins tightly in his hands.

"Are you ready?" He asked.

Darius nodded. He stepped out of the house and felt the sudden coolness in the air. His confusion must have been evident on his face because Hydarnes looked up at the sky and said, "I believe it is a sign that we are on the right path. A welcome for the new king."

Darius smiled and looked at the moon with hope.

"It seems as though it is," Darius said and walked over to the post where his horse, Roshan, stood tied. As soon as Darius stepped closer, his Roshan moved his head into his owner's hands and allowed himself to be petted.

"Don't disappoint me, Roshan," Darius whispered and watched the horse's ear twitch in response.

"Let us go," Hydarnes said.

Together, the six made their way through the lands. Darius was anxious. He looked around but saw no sign of Oibares.

"Nervous?" Hydarnes asked as he rode forward beside him.

Darius immediately cast his eyes ahead and gently petted Roshan's neck.

"It is not up to me to decide, but rather my horse and the God above," he said.

Hydarnes nodded.

"Ahuramazda makes no mistake. The right man will be picked today," he said, then fell silent.

Only the sound of hooves resounded across the emptiness. Darius could see the moon begin to disappear. The day's break was close at hand, and the six Persians rode on, each lost in their thoughts.

Darius secretly cast his eyes in the bushes to see if Oibares was there but was only greeted by nothingness.

"He has done nothing," Darius thought to himself, a sense of defeat overcoming him.

Suddenly, Roshan nudged his head and slowed down. Darius looked at him, confused, then looked up.

"What is it?" He whispered, but before he could get off, Roshan sped off into the horizon, neighing loudly as the sun came up.

A smile crept up on Darius's face. Then he turned back to see the rest of the nobles standing. He pulled on the reigns to calm his horse, and as soon as he did, loud thunder broke in the distance. The clap of the clouds and lightning resounded over the horizon.

"God has chosen the king," Hydarnes whispered as his eyes opened wide at the sight of the thunder. It was as though the heavens were inaugurating the welcome of the new King of Persia.

Darius looked at the rustling in the distance and saw Oibares holding the reins of the mare that Roshan was mated with. Darius smiled, then laughed, then looked toward the others riding forward. Quickly they leaped off their horses and kneeled before the king. Together, they rode back into the city, with one being granted the stature of the king. Darius looked at the people who slowly walked out of their houses at the break of day and then watched as he made his way towards the palace.

"All hail, Darius, King of Persia!" Oibares chanted.

Those who stood around murmured, and then a cheer broke out. Slowly, the rest of them joined in, following the great king to the palace. From this time onward, Darius' kingdom was set. As he walked through the city during his inauguration, he went up to a stone carving. He looked at the man mounted on top of it with a hammer and nail. He smiled as he read the inscription. It read:

"Darius, son of Hystaspes, by the aid of his good horse and his good groom Oibares, got himself the kingdom of the Persians."

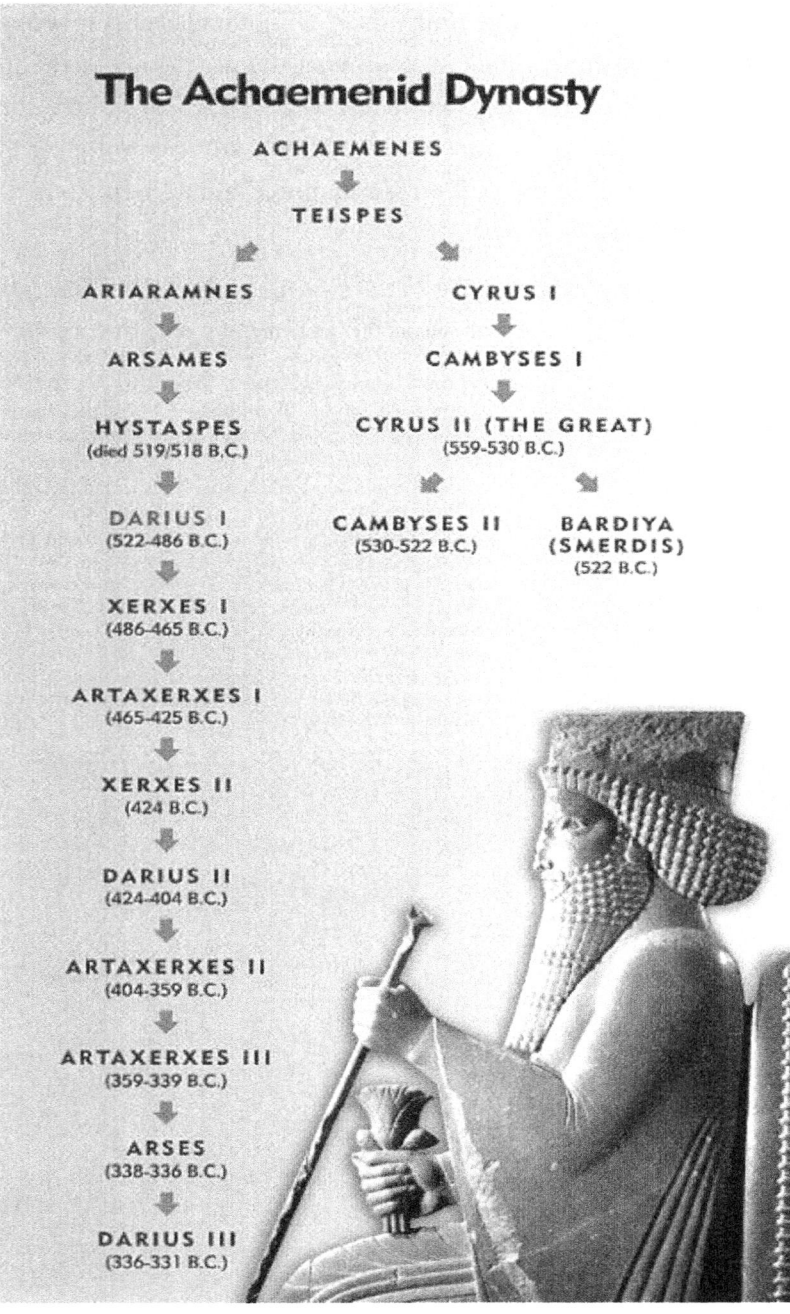

The Achaemenid Dynasty

ACHAEMENES

TEISPES

ARIARAMNES

ARSAMES

HYSTASPES
(died 519/518 B.C.)

DARIUS I
(522-486 B.C.)

XERXES I
(486-465 B.C.)

ARTAXERXES I
(465-425 B.C.)

XERXES II
(424 B.C.)

DARIUS II
(424-404 B.C.)

ARTAXERXES II
(404-359 B.C.)

ARTAXERXES III
(359-339 B.C.)

ARSES
(338-336 B.C.)

DARIUS III
(336-331 B.C.)

CYRUS I

CAMBYSES I

CYRUS II (THE GREAT)
(559-530 B.C.)

CAMBYSES II
(530-522 B.C.)

BARDIYA
(SMERDIS)
(522 B.C.)

Statue of Darius The Great at Persepolis

Chapter 6: Atusa

Darius stood in the veranda and looked up at the stars. He smiled at the beauty that engulfed the sky. His mind raced with thoughts of how his luck had unfolded.

When Darius won the challenge, there was still a lot that had to be done. The preparations for the new king were yet to be made, and Persia had to accept Darius as the successor. The rules were set, and so, being part of the Achaemenian dynasty and lacking royal blood, he would not be granted permission to rule.

When Darius had ridden back with the five closes behind him, Otanes awaited him in the palace walls. The moment Darius laid eyes on him, he knew there was something amiss. The otherwise smiling face that he had hoped to see was replaced by a solemn expression.

"Otanes, what is it, friend?" Darius said, jumping off his horse and listening to the others following close behind. He handed the leash to his faithful Oibares, who smirked secretly at him.

"There are still matters of grave importance. You must come inside," Otanes said. Darius turned back to look at the confused expressions of the other five who had now stepped off their horses. He turned back to Otanes and followed him into the palace.

They made their way to the great hall. Darius suddenly stopped at the sight of two much older and nobler men sitting at the table. Otanes went and sat by them and then held out his hand, gesturing Darius to take a seat as well.

Darius recognized the men. He had often seen them accompanying Cambyses and guiding his plans. He took a seat and then glanced at each of the men expectantly.

"Word has reached us of your challenge, Darius, and how the Ahuramazda himself was in favor of you gaining the monarchy," one of them said.

Darius smiled at him, waiting for him to continue.

"It is true that you won your right to rule. However, it is clearly stated that you need to be royal blood to receive that right," the man said, sending a wave of disbelief toward Darius. He looked at them, then at Otanes as the murmurs began from the other men.

"There is none sharing the royal blood. They are all dead, in case you have forgotten. I slay the last one claiming treason and pretending to be the son of Cyrus," Darius said, his voice firm. A hint of a smile touched the old man's face, and he looked to the other man.

"I have not forgotten, it was a very noble thing you did, for all of Persia," he said. "However, that is why we are here." He turned to the other man, who cleared his throat.

"Darius, the decision of who is to rule falls on our Queen, Queen Atusa, daughter of Cyrus the Great. We had consulted her on the matters, and it seems she is taken by your gesture for her kingdom. Bound by law, it seems your only chance to rule is through the marriage with Queen Atusa. We have consulted her, and she has agreed. What say you, Darius?" He said.

Darius was suddenly aware of being the center of attention. All eyes in the room were directed at him. He had heard a great deal about Queen Atusa. She was a strong woman educated in matters of law and land. She was also the wife of Cambyses. Her beauty was immeasurable, spoken of throughout the land. He turned to Otanes and leaned in.

"I am already married, with children, and promised to your daughter as well," he said, looking into his eyes.

Otanes straightened his back and looked at the advisors sitting across from them.

"It would seem that Darius and I have some matters to discuss. If you excuse us, we would have your answer in only a few moments," Otanes said.

They nodded in agreement. Otanes stood up and walked out of the room with Darius behind him. They reached the veranda and walked side by side in silence at first. They listened to the birds chirping in the trees. Darius stopped and turned to Otanes, noticing a smile on his face.

"You have a mighty fine woman in your midst, Darius," Otanes said.

Darius looked at him in confusion. "Have you met her?" He asked.

"Only once, but never in my years have I seen a woman like that. She is a true testament to her mother, Cassandane, carrying her beauty and grace. Her thoughts in matters of politics set us all aside," Otanes said, surprising Darius.

"But aside from her beauty, it seems you have a good chance through this marriage. You see, not only will you attain the right to rule, but your children will also gain nobility," Otanes explained.

"It seems true and a just decision to make," Darius said, almost to himself. "Yet, there is much to think about." He gave Otanes a look. Understanding his unspoken words, the older man nodded.

"I shall notify the others to wait," Otanes said, turning around and walking into the palace.

As soon as he reached the Great Hall, a sudden silence spread in the room. It was only then that he realized Darius was walking behind him with confidence marked on his face. He stepped aside to let him enter.

"I have accepted the conditions to legitimatize my monarchy," Darius said.

The advisors smiled as the others cheered. "We shall inform the Queen. The marriage shall commence in a day's time," they said, taking their leave. The men stood up and walked out of the palace, readying themselves to welcome a new course in Persia's history.

Statue of Queen Atusa

The marriage took place and then the ceremony of the inauguration of the king. Darius addressed his people, looking at the hope that filled the land. He stood with the group of seven behind him, and his wives watched from the private chambers in the palace.

"Sire, the queen requests for you in her chamber," a servant said, stealing away Darius's thoughts and the first moment of silence as a king.

Darius nodded at him and then turned his attention back to the sky. A single star shined bright, lighting up the otherwise clear sky. "Thank you, Gods, for granting me this position to rule as the great king. I shall do everything in my power to bring peace and prosperity and never let the people go hungry," he whispered.

The wind blew past him as if Ahuramazda had accepted him. Darius smiled and then turned back into the palace. He walked past long corridors until he reached his chamber, where the candles were still lit. He stepped inside and looked at the woman standing by the bed, lighting a candle. She turned around as soon as she heard his footsteps with a smile slowly bracing her face.

"Welcome, King Darius," she said in a sultry voice.

"I see that I made the right decision choosing you. I hope you will not disappoint," she added, smiling.

Queen Atusa

Darius looked on, mesmerized by her beauty. The orange glow from the candles fell on her face, making it glow ethereally. Her eyes were green and glimmered with hope, and her long sandy hair fell over her shoulders.

When Darius looked upon her, he thought of the Persian Aphrodite, Anahita. Her name meant mighty, fertility, and immaculate. In the Zoroastrian belief, Anahita is a strong, beautiful maiden traveling on a chariot pulled by four horses, sleet, wind, cloud, and rain. While Darius was not Zoroastrian himself, he still had seen the numerous statues built of her, showing clearly the power she held. Anahita was a female Water Goddess of Birth, Fertility, and Womanhood. She was a Goddess responsible for taking care of women and protecting them, especially in childbirth.

Statue of Anahita

Statue of Anahita

Women of Persia took the Goddess Anahita as a symbol of purity, often representing water crystal clear water beds. Those who met the Queen often spoke of her voice resembling the clarity of the water, the calm, and the storm. She was timeless, taken by the old Persian believers, and was revered.

Anahita was calm, holding the sacredness of rivers and lakes. Atusa often read through the great scriptures to find Anahita described for her beauty, often speaking of her full breasts and virginity. Owning to what others often said about her, Atusa kept doves and peacocks, the sacred animals of Anahita.

The conquest of Babylon in the sixth century showed Anahita to display similar qualities to the Goddess Ishtar. That was when the people knew she was descended from Ishtar.

Anahita

Atusa was much like Anahita, with keen, intelligent eyes and red lips. Much like Anahita often dressed, Atusa adorned her body with a thin golden robe and large jewels glittering around her neck. She then took off her diamond tiara and placed it on the table. Smiling at Darius, she extended her hand.

"Queen Atusa, you are just as beautiful as Anahita." Slowly, she walked up to him, the cloth slipping off her shoulders and slowly falling to the floor.

He watched her, unable to turn from her beauty.

"Tell me, Darius, Do you truly believe yourself to be worthy of me? I am the daughter of Cyrus, after all. Wife of Cyrus' sons, the previous kings of Persia..." she said, circling him and tracing a finger on his face as she did. She studied him carefully.

"I am humbled in your presence, Queen Atusa. I am just a man granted the favor of the Gods, but I shall forever work to be worthy of you," he said softly, bowing his head to her as she stopped in front of him.

"Then now, I will be known as Atusa, the wife of Darius the Great, the new king of Persia," she whispered into his ear.

A smile slowly spread on Darius' face on hearing the words. His eyes looked ahead, but he slowly turned his head toward Atusa, who stood close to him, her face a breath away from his. She looked at him, studying his face, then smiled and backed away.

"Come, let us celebrate this victory and pray for the future of our kingdom," Atusa said. She picked up a goblet from the table, poured herself some wine, and then handed one goblet to Darius.

"There is still much to discuss..." Darius began.

Atusa raised her hand, walked up to him, lifted his hands to grasp the goblet, and gently ran a finger across his arms.

"Tonight is a night for celebrations, my king. Tomorrow, we shall take care of other matters," she said.

He smiled and downed his drink and then followed her into bed. The curtains fluttered with the wind, making the candles go out, replacing the silence with the moans of a new life.

Darius' eyes fluttered open at the sounds of birds chirping outside. The rays from the rising sun surrounded him, and he looked around at the empty room. Confused, he rose and was immediately surrounded by servants.

The servants ushered around him, some bringing him his robes, the rest taking him to the bath. Once he was ready, he was handed his sword and crown and then led toward the throne room where Queen Atusa stood with the rest of his wives in a line.

"Good morning, my king," Atusa bowed, as did the others.

He nodded at her, holding her gaze, and then looked toward his other wives. One of them was the daughter of Otanes, as was promised.

"Come, join us to break our fast," Atusa said and led him toward the dining hall.

The table was laden with food and fruits, and the servants rushed about with trays of delicacies. The wives all sat nearby, with Queen Atusa closest to the king.

Cassandane was the most beloved of Cyrus the Great's wives, and that had granted Atusa the preference she received from her father. Because of this, she was educated to the highest merit. Atusa was strong-willed, and her personality shone bright, demanding attention and respect.

As she sat next to Darius now, Atusa's eyes traveled to each woman on the table. She studied them all carefully. Being the wife of Cambyses and then Bardia, she had learned the works of aristocrats and courtiers, training herself in the political ways.

"Before we indulge in talks of the late king Cambyses' pursuits to Egypt, there is an important matter we must discuss," Queen Atusa said, sending a wave of silence across the room.

The women all stopped to watch her, then King Darius, who looked at Atusa in surprise.

"And what is that, my dear Queen?" He asked, his voice firm yet gentle.

"As you know, I had converted to the Zoroastrian religion long ago to help better understand my people and their needs. I request you, King Darius, to consider converting as well."

Darius slipped one grape into his mouth as his lips twitched into a smile. The indication paved the way for the rest of them to begin eating once again. As the others chatted amongst themselves, Atusa looked at him expectantly. It was not an easy decision to make, to let go of the years of religion that you knew and understood, and to adopt a new one. However, this was beneficial to the entire kingdom.

As Atusa sat by the king, her mind buzzed with the memories of when she had converted. She had stood in the temple, bowing in front of the Zoroaster, who chanted a prayer as he blessed her. Once he had finished his prayer, she was told to repeat it. The man had then helped her stand beside him in a temple filled with people, looking on to their Queen with newfound respect.

"She is converted to my Mazdyasna's beliefs," the Zoroaster had announced.

The room erupted into cheers and claps. Some people walked up to hug her while the guards held them back. Queen Atusa had still met some of her people and assured their safety.

"You see, it is not easy for me to renounce my God," Darius' words took her out of her attention.

"Indeed, it is a difficult task. I, too, had not gone forward with it were it not for my people," Atusa replied, her keen eyes watching him closely.

"Yes, the people. I shall consider it," Darius said.

Atusa returned to the plate in front of her as her mind reeled with thoughts. She had felt the winds of change long ago. Now, everything that Darius did was a test for her until he could prove that he genuinely cared for the betterment of Persia itself, instead of just looking at the fame he would receive. A conversion, in her mind, was the biggest test he would have to take.

As the day began to sink away, Atusa made her way to the veranda, where she often sat to align her thoughts. She stepped out, and the slave girls bowed out of the way, then whispered to each other as they often did about her beauty.

Silence had spread across the palace as some of the wives had gone to their cities. The king remained here, overlooking the plans laid about the siege that Cambyses had started. Queen Atusa would ordinarily join them, even though some of the nobles felt it unwise. However, today, she felt as though she could take some time to herself.

As Atusa sat on the bench, she picked up a flower and studied its petals. A soft pair of footsteps sounded behind her, and she jumped to get away but breathed in relief at the sight of Darius. He smiled at Atusa's attempts to hide her blush.

"Should you not be in the war room with the nobles?" She asked.

"I sent them away. It seems I have not been able to properly get to know my Queen," he said, taking the flower from her hand and placing it in her hair. As he saw her in the daylight, he still couldn't believe how beautiful she was.

Amongst a lineage of Achaemenid empresses in Persia, Atusa was regarded with notions of beauty and purity. She was a magnanimous figure in the empire, a symbol of the gods' finest manifestations of the human race.

Atusa's beauty was a sight to revel in. Tales of it grew popular across the empire, impressing the hearts of nobles and peasants alike. The kingdom was in awe of their empress. From servants not helping but blinking to slave girls murmuring in wonderment of her long, silky, black hair to diplomats easing their strides and throwing words of their own accord in the marvel of her beauty, Atusa's beauty affected everyone.

Tales of Atusa's magnificence grew in Persia. She was the closest being to their beautiful Goddess Aphrodite, who holds the same stature as Venus, Isis, Nana, and Ishtar. She was grace if grace could live, breathe, and exist in an enchanting show of beauty. She was regarded as the throbbing heart and a beacon of splendor in a rather grim empire of Persia.

Queen Atusa

Darius sat down, placing a hand on the empty seat beside him. Atusa took a seat and looked up in the sky.

"There has been a question plaguing my mind. I do not wish to offend you by it," Darius began and looked toward her.

When she nodded her approval, he continued.

"Cambyses was your brother, was he not? It is not a common practice in Persia to marry within the family, especially in royal blood. How did it come about?" He asked cautiously. He could see Atusa smile ever so slightly and the look down at her hands.

"Cambyses was a great king. Some say he was mad, but I knew the power he had and the greatness in the strategies he used. I could almost see our father in him sometimes," Atusa said in a low voice. She then looked at Darius.

"At first, I had thought he cared for me as a brother cares for a sister, but when he confessed his love for me, I was shocked. I could not believe his words, and even if I did, I knew he could not do anything, knowing it was not practiced. I made him a deal. I told him that if he was able to prove to me that he could, in fact, marry me, then I would do so."

Atusa sighed deeply and continued, "His love for me grew by the day, and it made me love him, too. Keeping my words at heart, the very next day, he gathered all the judges of Persia and then forced them to legalize the marriage, making it legitimate. Fearing for their lives, they did legalize it, but in turn, he was labeled the Mad King."

She looked away and added, "His death...it was painful for me. He was a great ruler, but what they said about him was not true. Everything he did, he did for the people."

"He was a great king indeed. To conquer Egypt was one of his greatest accomplishments. Were he alive, I know he would have made an example of Bardia," Darius said. Upon hearing the name, Atusa squinted in disgust.

"May the Gods never let Bardia be in peace," she said, the anger and disgust apparent in her voice.

"They will now. Treason is not accepted by the Gods as well," he said fiercely. He took a deep breath and looked up at the sky. The dying sun cast a beautiful purple glow of colors across the sky.

Darius then turned toward Atusa. "I have decided I will accept the Zoroastrian belief," he finally said.

Atusa's head whipped up at him in disbelief. A smile crept over her face. Then she let out a laugh of pure happiness.

"Truly?" She asked, her eyes glimmering with happiness.

Darius nodded happily.

"It will benefit you, you shall see," she said.

"I have no doubt," he said, smiling.

While Darius did not know it, Atusa was happy for more than just his acceptance. She was pleased that she had made the right decision. Now, she was confident he was the man to rule the kingdom. She was happy for a new life she was going to lead. She was determined that together she and Darius would achieve greatness beyond comparison.

Darius and Atusa

Chapter 7: Zoroastrian

Darius was ready to embrace Zoroastrianism, but there was still a lot that he had to do. As he walked out of his chamber at the first break of light, his mind was still muddled with thoughts. He walked through the halls, watching as the freckles of light slowly began to enter through the windows.

"Convert to a different religion," he thought and took a deep breath.

"But I don't even know the first thing about Zoroastrianism. Never took the time to learn," he thought as he stood by one of the windows and looked out over the horizon. A soft breeze made its way to him, whipping his hair back. His robe slowly fluttered with it.

He could see a bell ringing in the distance and a few people making their way to the temple. He remembered Cyrus had built a library not far from the temple where he had kept all the important documents. As the thought occurred to him, he turned to walk out of the palace. Immediately, the guards stood alert and began to follow him.

"Stay here. I will return," Darius said. Confused, the guards lowered and went back to their positions.

Oibares immediately ran over to him and handed him his horse's reins. "Would you like me to accompany you, my liege?" He asked.

Darius smiled at him and shook his head. He got up on his horse and rode off toward the library. As soon as he reached the library, he saw one of the temple leaders standing guard. At the sight of the king, the man bowed in front of him. "Please, rise," he said, putting a hand on the man's shoulder and helping him up. "You are the temple leader. Must you not be at the temple?" Darius asked, confused.

"Cyrus had left the library in the care of the leaders. I come here once a day to see if everything is in order. How might I be of service, my liege?" The man said, putting his hands together and walking side by side with the king.

"I wish to know more about your religion, Zoroastrianism. My wife, the Queen, has informed me of her conversion. It intrigued me to learn more."

The man turned to him with a smile bracing his face. "It seems you are a learner. Indeed, Queen Atusa's conversion was a privilege to us all. She is the epitome of a true leader," he said.

"Yes, she is." Darius smiled as they walked into the building made of clay walls with torches mounted on all the walls. The large hall lay ahead of them, filled with tables and scrolls.

Prophet Zoroastar

"Our Prophet Zoroaster (or Zarathustra) had brought us news of the one God we call Ahura Mazda. It was through him that we are all alive today and have the lands and the water and the sky," he said. His voice rose with excitement as he spoke to his king about Ahura Mazda. He walked up to one of the tables and opened a scroll. He put it in front of Darius, who leaned to look at it.

"He is omniscient, omnipotent, omnipresent, and impossible for us humans to conceive. His power and knowledge surpass all the lands. No one can change Him, and it is only through Him that all life was created. Through him, we have happiness and all the goodness in the world."

He paused and looked at his king. Darius nodded to show he was listening. The man continued speaking.

"We believe that everything created by Ahura Mazda is pure and should be treated with respect. The trees, rivers, animals, air, even people of other religions."

Darius nodded, his eyes gazing out toward the garden from the window. There, another man was kneeling on the ground and planting a seed. Beside him, lambs ate the grass and jumped around.

"I once traveled with Cambyses right after he had taken over Egypt. Those people believed, through the words of travelers, that we worship fire. It is not true. We merely carry it as a beacon of light through the darkness, just as Azda Mazda guides us. Fire is pure. It shows God's light and wisdom that fills out the land," he said.

Darius looked up at him. "You have a temple..." he began.

"Yes, the Agiary or the Fire Temple. It is there that we gather to worship together. We read from the Avesta, our Holy Book," the man said, picking up a stack of papers bound together in leather. He carefully placed it on the table and ran his fingers through it.

As the light from the sun lit up the temple and fell on the book, Darius saw the engravings. He slowly caressed it, feeling the soft leather against his fingers.

"It is the work of God. The opening prayer," the man said and then recited it.

Without knowing it, Darius stared at him, mesmerized by the odd way he sang the words. He felt his heart leap with every word. "What does it mean?" Darius asked once the man had finished.

Looking at the glaze of interest in his eyes, the man smiled and told him it was a prayer to give thanks and welcome the reader to the words of Prophet Zoroaster.

"We pray several times a day, but there is no time. We only pray to give thanks and seek forgiveness for our mischief."

"What of the Avesta?" Darius asked.

"Oh, yes, it is one of the scriptures that we hold close to us. No trouble shall befall it and no harm shall come to us," he said and opened it to see the writings of charcoal.

"This contains the Gathas, the seventeen hymns that Zoroaster wrote himself. They said that when he first sang it, the dark clouds eclipsing the land for months split apart and allowed the sun to shine onto him. We sing this at the Agiary on the nights of devotion. It allows us to believe that someday, the problems and divisions will come to an end."

Darius absorbed all that in silence. Never had he seen someone talk so passionately about religion. He could sense himself wanting to learn more about it and did not deem it fit to interrupt the temple leader in his quest to teach Darius more about Zoroastrianism.

"Would you like to learn more about Zoroaster?" The temple leader asked, smiling as he closed the scripture softly, a cloud of dust lifting from it.

Darius nodded affirmatively. He gazed up to look at him in hopes the temple leader would continue speaking.

"Many people believe Zoroaster to be a god, but that is a flaw in their understanding. Zoroaster, like you and I, is nothing but a wise mortal. Possibly the wisest of us all, but a mortal after all."

For a moment, Darius did not follow, but he tried to ignore all the questions that rushed through his mind. It seemed as though he had run out of words. The temple leader sensed his confusion as he walked a little in his direction.

"At the age of thirty, Zoroaster had a divine vision whilst bathing in a river during a pagan purification rite. On the bank of the river, he saw a 'Shining Being' made of light which revealed himself as *Vohu Manah*, which means Good Mind." The man explained.

"How could you know all that?" Darius asked intriguingly. He knew kingdoms and battles better than anyone, but religion and sanctity were something he lacked the understanding of. He did not shy away from letting the temple leader know.

"From the writings and teachings of Zoroaster," replied the man.

"Vohu Manah led Zoroaster to the presence of *Ahura Mazda* (God) and five other radiant beings, which are called the *Amesha Spentas* (Holy Immortals). This was the first of several visions, in which Zoroaster saw Ahura Mazda and his Amesha Spentas. During each vision, he asked many questions. The answers given to Zoroaster are the foundations of the Zoroastrian religion." The man answered as he went back to teach Darius about the fundamentals.

Darius could see the flickering sunlight through the window, clouds trying to comprise the power of rays every chance they got but failing to hold them inside. Darius thought of himself as the rays, too, trying to peak through his cloud of intrigue and confusion so he could shine his brightest. He shifted his attention away from the window and back to the man.

"How do you read it?" Asked Darius, pointing toward the book still in the man's hand. His curiosity seemed to please the temple leader.

"The Vendidad, Visperad, and Yasna are always recited together, and the Gathas are hymns that we sing."

It was a shared sentiment amongst the public to be affectionate toward one's empire, but he did not think it was possible to be attracted to something unseen. However, this feeling of a greater power stunned him.

"How could I sense God's existence if I don't see him," questioned Darius.

"We believe that man can know God through his Divine Attributes and six Amesha Spentas; *Vohu Manah* - Good mind and useful purpose, *Asha Vahishta* - Truth and righteousness, *Spenta Ameraiti* - Holy devotion, serenity and loving-kindness, *Khashathra Vairya* - Power and just rule, *Hauravatat* - Wholeness and health and, *Ameretat* - Long life and immortality.

Darius knew all about the sorts of people and recognized all these attributes. He wished everyone was as dedicated as the temple leader was for a noble cause.

"It may seem impossible for us to comprehend at first, my king, but it is the truth," the man said as he spoke once again. He held a passion for Ahura Mazda and it was evident from both his action and speech.

"What about the evil that rots our empire? The bloodshed and the people who die because of prejudice," Darius asked. He could never understand why, if there was a fair higher power responsible for creating everything abundant and majestic could stand by and tolerate all this mayhem and chaos.

"Evil has been there since the inception of time. Like all great leaders, God has a nemesis too. Ahura Mazda," the man said as he paused to study Darius' face to see if his distress and confusion were cleared.

"Could you tell me more?" Darius asked respectfully.

"It would be my pleasure," responded the temple leader as he continued speaking.

"Ah, you see, unlike Ahura Mazda, who is perfect and abides in Heaven, Angra Mainyu dwells in the depths of Hell. Angra Mainyu means destructive spirit. He is the originator of death and all that is evil in the world. When a person dies, they will go to Heaven or Hell depending on their deeds during their lifetime," the man went on making reasonable explanations.

Statue of Prophet Zoroastar

Darius never thought of himself as a spiritual leader, but he understood that a man could not always be where he wanted to be. He still ended up where he belonged. Darius knew he was destined to be here, standing in this temple and learning about the teaching of Zoroaster.

"Very well then, I'll take your leave now," Darius said as he began to walk back.

"You may," He replied. "But, your place is here with us, spreading the beautiful message of Zoroaster and the belief in Ahura Mazda." He looked at Darius, praying for his consent. Darius had no doubts in his mind. After his talk with Atusa the previous night and now learning about Zoroaster, he knew what and who he believed in. Darius nodded approvingly with a smile.

"I must go myself," he replied without giving much away.

"This is God's will," the man instructed Darius. He looked at him, all ready to leave.

Darius said a silent prayer of thanks to the Ahura Mazda as he walked through the open door behind him with new desire and motives for his nation.

Chapter 8: Military Campaigns

The news of Darius' conversion spread, and soon, all of Persia was more than happy to welcome their new king. Now that the people accepted him, he had bigger plans in mind.

As Darius had always hoped, he was ruling the Persian Empire at its zenith. He had the kingdom under his power, and all the area was his to have control over, but that did not stop him from wanting more. His military conquest expanded Persia's boundaries, but with expansion came rebuttals, and with rebuttals came scrapes for him and his command.

The new emperor did not allow his gaze to settle. It was not every day that kings faced such hostility and opposition. However, Darius' selection as king was surrounded by controversy since the day he was chosen.

Chaos began to run deep within the land of the new king's realm. In every corner that Darius took under his wing, people opposed the Liege. Darius could not have been more worried. He had hoped his rule would unite the whole territory, but he could not have been more wrong. Darius needed to know the people that bordered him were worth his conviction. Hence, he called an assembly of all the vital folks.

Darius was met with campaigning against not only his regime but also cyclical rebuttals. He knew he had to fight to hold on to his leadership. As revolts broke out across his kingdom, he resorted to military crusades.

Once the individuals started to appear, Darius instructed his men to bring them a fort. He was sitting with his council of men in his chamber. The general clapped his hands, indicating that someone was here to meet Darius.

It was highly unlikely that anyone's arrival was important enough to disrupt the meeting of the council. Everyone in the hall sat there quietly, staring at the dark entrance waiting for the culprit responsible for bringing the gathering to a standstill.

A grim-looking man who appeared wavered and filthy emerged from the entrance of the chamber door barefooted. The man had not come for the council. He had come with a warning that would shake the king's trust in his regime. The vacillated-looking man claimed to be an envoy from Babylon.

"My apologies, sire! I do not mean to interrupt your meeting, but I'm afraid I have some tragic news for you," the man said as he gasped for air. It looked like he had run all the way here. The man looked around, getting an idea of just how many men were in attendance. He could not recognize anyone, for he was not native. He established, from his understanding, that everyone important in the kingdom was present. He looked around at the room hesitantly at the men looking at him. He shifted on his feet and paused.

"Out with it, young man," one of the men sitting near Darius exclaimed as the council grew impatient.

An uncomfortable silence rose from the depths of the messenger as he carefully worded what he had come in to say.

"I have news of a revolt in Babylon against Liege Darius," exclaimed the man.

The news was enough to send everyone in a roar of divergence. Darius was prepared for a day like this. This information was not shocking. It was not the first time the Babylonians tried to upset the regime. Nidintu-Bêl led the first attempt, but Darius violently suppressed it.

"Is that all you came to say, or do you have anything else to add," asked Darius in all seriousness.

"There is a man who claims to be the son of Nabonidus; he says, '*I am Nebuchadnezzar, the son of Nabonidus*,' and the Babylonians believe him. People are revolting against you and your rule. They consider him their king," the man said, almost ominously.

Nebuchadnezzar was a nobleman of Urartian (Armenian) descent who had seized power in Babylon. The leader of the revolt was Arakha, the son of a man by the name of Haldita, but Arakha assumed the name Nebuchadnezzar and claimed to be a son of Nabonidus, Babylon's last independent king. Arakha was not a native Babylonian, but he adjusted the name to gain the trust of his people.

Babylon

The Babylonians trusted the name and they quickly gave their support to Nebuchadnezzar IV. They assumed he was the one who would free their land from King Darius.

Nebuchadnezzar IV, like his antecedents, did not accept King Darius as king, nor did he plead his allegiance with the new rule. He wanted power for himself and there were many in the land who followed a pursuit. Nebuchadnezzar caused a division. He wanted Darius to know he was no king for him and his people, and that title only belonged to him. Soon after becoming the state's ruler, he initiated to his people that he would lead a revolt against the Persian Achaemenid Empire.

"And why have you come to tell us this now?" A man amidst the council inquired about the envoy. It was dubious for individuals to turn over their territories no matter how much they differed from it. Allegiance ran deep within everyone's blood.

"I came to warn you as I take no pleasure in watching a city burn," the man replied. He knew he was risking his life by telling them this information. The murmurs in the chamber had grown louder with each sentence the man spoke.

"Enough!" The Darius roared, rising from his seat, his voice thick with irritation.

Silence fell as everyone understood the momentousness of the issue. There was peace in the hall for the next few minutes to come, but it was no ordinary peace. It was the kind of peace envisioned before a storm. It looked like the atmosphere had adapted to the seriousness of the issue, too, as everything became silent. The wind stopped blowing, the birds stopped singing, and the men sat still.

"Does anyone of you men present in the council before I have any notions of dealing with this?" Asked Darius before he announced his verdict.

No one answered. They were scared to challenge the king's plan; hence they thought it was better for them to remain silent. No one dared to say anything to obstruct what the King was about to say. He was the wisest of them all.

Upon Darius' succession as the rightful heir to the kingdom, the other conspirators who had helped Darius attain power stipulated for free admission to the king at all times. Amongst this pavilion of men was a man whom Darius had handpicked to be his army's general. His name was Intaphrenes. He was a colossal man that Darius trusted. Darius knew he would be perfect to lead the charge. Intraphenes was not only bestowed with the responsibility of Darius's army, but he was also his Bow Carrier and a top military commander. If anyone could finish the uprising, it was Intraphenes.

Darius trusted him enough to instruct him to lead the charge against the rebels in Babylon. Darius stood up and called upon him. A man rose from his seat and presented himself to the king in an affable demeanor.

"My king, tell me what it is that you want me to do?" Asked Intaphrenes in an attempt to break the silence.

Darius turned his attention toward him and began to speak. His voice was loud enough for everyone present in the hall to hear.

"A king without a kingdom is no king. I want you to go and protect my kingdom as well as my honor, Intaphrenes," Darius spoke directly to the head of his army.

The gravity of the situation required urgency. As fast as Darius dealt with this uprising, the easier it would be to contain before a severe threat of a revolution knocked on their doors.

"Let this information sink in your hollow skull carefully, Intaphrenes," Darius said as he warned Intaphrenes for his journey to Babylon.

"I do not want you to come back unless the uprising has settled. Do whatever is in your power to contain it. Go, smite that Babylonian host who does not acknowledge me," Darius continued.

Darkness crawled toward Persia that night as Darius laid awake in thought. This was not the first time Babylonians had tried to cause an uprising. For more than a century, the region had obstructed anyone who was in command. This time it was no different. Their plan to refute the king was soon to be met with ordnance and muscle.

In King Darius' regime, this was their second attempt to refute the kingdom. The Babylonian revolt began in less than a year after the unsuccessful revolt of Nabonidus, and like his predecessor, Nebuchadrezzar, the new king, was not afraid of conflict.

His strategy was orthodox. He was to use the same regnal name the people trusted and as his predecessor wished for. He had to do so to align his own rebellion against the Persians.

Babylon

Intaphrenes, with a sizable Persian army, traveled to Babylon and placed the city under siege. The future now seemed even more ambiguous for the Darius regime. The fear of the kingdom being overhauled was looming on top of Darius' head.

A dark cloud of uncertainty hung around for days after King Darius' army had reached Babylon. They were met with resistance and a great deal of struggle. The coup seemed to have no end in near sight.

It had been over a year with no resolutions amongst the Persians and the Babylonians. Intaphrenes and his army's siege seemed futile. The trusted man of King Darius had not been able to get the results the regime had hoped for, and with no effect, the strategy to send a militia of thousands of men to Babylon looked ineffective.

The king was desperate and impatient. He asked Ahura Mazda for help. If anyone could help the king at this moment of uncertainty, it was his belief in a higher power. At that moment, there was a man by the name of Zopyrus. He was the son of Megabyzus, who had been with Darius when he killed the Magian.

Darius was a shrewd leader who had come up with another plot to come out on top this time and gain access to the city. It was after almost 18 months of no result, he called on Zopyrus to meet him.

"I did not think the siege would last this long," Darius said as he looked visibly worried.

Zopyrus looked down, waiting for his instructions to handle the matter.

"I want you to do something to help us resolve this," Darius said as he went on.

"It's not easy, and you may get hurt, but it is what the time requires you do, Zopyrus."

"You do not have to keep persisting me, my liege. I have not done my part yet, and I am happy to go there and be of any help I can be to you and the kingdom no matter how long it takes," Zopyrus responded approvingly.

The advisory then explained and helped Zopyrus build a strategy. They instructed him to cut off his ears and nose and to Babylon in hopes of baffling them with a story about how Darius punished Zopyrus when he disagreed with proving his allegiance to his regime.

That is precisely what Zopyrus did exactly. He mutilated his own body in hopes of having defeated the besieged city. Unaware of the plan Darius had set out Zopyrus for, Nabonidus did not take long to grant him access to come to take refuge in Babylon. He trusted his story to be accurate, and that is precisely what the Persian army had hoped for.

Zopyrus, once he went into the city, artfully arranged to open the city gates on a stormy night. It allowed the Persian troops to enter the town under cover of darkness and sandstorm.

The sun was only a quarter of its way up when the Persian army finally took the city as Intaphrenes marched with the army unto Babylon. The warriors paraded into the street of Babylon. They were ordered by Intraphenes to take any man alive who refused to pledge their allegiance to King Darius.

The state had finally been bare for Darius and his men to take control. When news reached Darius, he rejoiced. "Ahura Mazda brought me help. Intaphrenes overthrew the Babylonians and brought over the people unto me," Darius said as he thanked his God. That was when he finally seemed to comprehend his conquest.

Immortals Relief at Persepolis

The circumstances were favorable for Darius and his men. Now, by means of this, they were able to access the city. Darius the Great was able to forecast his victory. The general that hearkened his army was there to defeat those who dared to rebel against him and his mighty rule.

Intraphenes walked toward the great battle with a large army behind him. They had gained access to the city that had kept The Great Darius awake for months. He stood face to face with the enemy, preparing himself for the death that would spread the land. With one strike of his sword, the butchery of the rebels would start.

Quick as lightning, the roar of war rose, and the clash of metal resounded in the area. There was nothing but rosy streets. The city was red with the blood of the rebels.

He shouted commands and invectives down to the men of his army, "Spare no one that rebukes my king, kill them all!" Intraphenes's loud booming voiced echoed as he killed any man who came in his sight.

The sight of the Arakha and his men pleading and crying made Darius' men laugh with pride.

"Let one be made an example, for he who campaigns against the king has to die," Intraphenes said as he stood in Babylon.

There were carnage and bloodshed, and no life was spared. Intraphenes was functioning under his king's strict instructions to leave no man alive, except those who arranged this coup. He wanted them to be captured.

After almost 18 months, Babylon was under the control of Darius and his army. On the twenty-second day of the month, Markâsanaš *(27 November)*, they seized that Arakha, who called himself Nebuchadnezzar, and the men who were his chief followers.

As soon as Babylon was seized, Darius ordered Arakha and his chief followers to be brought to Babylon justice. Darius decreed his punishment upon him and Arakha's men.

"Let that Arakha and the men who were his chief followers be crucified in Babylon!" He said.

Darius wanted to set an example for everyone who supported these agitators. His demand was completed soon enough when the Arakha and his followers died a painful death after the fall of their violent coup.

This was the last time someone in Babylon tried to create an uprising after Darius and his army succeeded in subduing Babylon's revolt the second time.

Upon the return of Intaphrenes, he wanted to resolve the relationship he had with Darius. In hopes of meeting him and regaining more autocratic powers, he went straight to the palace and, having business to transact with Darius, he wished to enter the palace.

An agreement was made when the seven coconspirators murdered Guamata. If any of the conspirators visited the king unannounced, provided that he was not in bed with a woman, he would need no permission; and given this when Intaphrenes came to visit Darius, he expected to meet him on his own without being interrupted or needing permission. But to his surprise, that was not what happened.

As soon as Intaphrenes came to see Darius, he was met with resistance and asked to send his name. Intaphrenes refused to have his name sent in by a messenger.

"It is my right to walk in and meet with Darius. I do not need yours or his permission to walk through the halls of this building," Intaphrenes exclaimed as he claimed it was his right, as one of the seven, to walk straight in.

"The king is with a woman," the guards informed him, reassuring his doubt that Darius was, in fact, with a woman at the time.

"I do not believe you. I must go see the king at this very instance!" He said. The multiple resistance to his entry was making him irritated and furious.

"This is only an excuse to keep me out." Intaphrenes thought. Enraged, he drew his scimitar and, in one swift movement, cut off the guard's ears and noses. As blood spilled and the anguished cries rang out, he threaded them on his horse's strap and tied the belt around their necks.

"Go!" He yelled as he slapped his horses, making them drag out. It wasn't long after that news reached Darius and the men came to him bloodied and broken. They explained the reason for their plight.

"He would not take no for an answer and did not believe us when we told him the truth," they cried in pain.

Darius was conscious of the nature of the other five conspirators. He worried about any plotting against his regime from the hands of his own, especially Intaphrenes. He did not take his actions lightly, and this event at once suggested to the king the alarming possibility of a new conspiracy.

Thinking that his six former accomplices might all be in this business together, he sent each of them in turn and sounded them to see if they approved of what Intaphrenes had done.

Darius himself wanted to confirm his doubts before it was too late. "Do you perceive what Intraphenes has done to my guards to be fitting?"

It was evident that he was plotting a plan in his mind. Intraphenes had not come in celebration. He had come to claim my seat at the throne. Darius thought.

He sat back on his throne and scratched his beard, lost in thought. "My husband, why don't you send men to each of the Nobel men?" Queen Atusa asked him as she grabbed his hand.

The gentle ray of light lingered in the empty room. Darius took a deep breath and nodded.

"And so I shall," he said, calling one of the guards over to him.

"Gather five of your best men," he instructed them and looked around.

"Bring them to me. I shall see to it that the job is done." He turned to look at his wife, who nodded in agreement.

Darius gathered his most trustworthy men around him and focused on each one of them. "Ask all the Nobel men as soon as you see them about the plans of Intraphenes. They may be wary of unforeseen inquiring. But do not return without an answer. If anyone of them is reluctant, bring them to me," commanded Darius. He was going to make sure his regime was uncontested and free of connivers.

"As you command, our king," the men obeyed and turned. Their footsteps were softening away as they left the palace.

Darius' men set out to find Otanes, Gobryas, Hydarnes, Megabyzus, and Aspathines – the five other men who assisted him in killing Gaumata in the fortress of Sikayauvati. Darius knew that if their answered differed, it would be a definitive sign that an invasion was at play.

As the darkness of the night took over everything, the air grew calmer and the surroundings were still. Ten of Darius' men set out to meet the five Nobel men. They set out in the dark to avoid suspicion and any troubling eyes.

Darius had sent ten men so two of his men could question each of the Nobel men at the same time. He feared anyone of the five men suspected that Darius knew they might rebel earlier than expected.

Without much uncertainty, all of them were cautious of this unprecedented event occurring before their eyes. When the men showed up on their doors, the shock registered on their faces.

"He suspects us of stabbing him in his back?" They asked, shocked.

"Intraphenes cannot take the throne without your help. If you're wise, you'll make certain that King Darius knows of any such plans." The two men said to Otanes. Their eyes locked to his response to study any expression that might give away his allegiance to Intraphenes.

"Are you, or anyone of you, in support of what Intraphenes had done to Darius' guard?" They inspected, a stern look on their face.

Otanes was alarmed. He didn't dare to say anything. He silently shook his head, but this was not enough to make Darius's loyal servants trust him.

"Tell my king that I have no hand in any of this," Otanes finally managed to say as he wiped his sweaty palms across his forehead.

Just like him, the rest denied the accusations. They shook their head at every question the men asked them. Their innocence was no longer suspected. If Intraphenes had planned anything, they were not involved in any of them.

Darius' men returned one by one and informed him of their intentions. He shook his head in disagreement. He was not yet convinced of their allegiance. He sat inside the comfort of his room on his bed, all alone. He had asked his guards to bring him one of the men who went to question Hydarnes. Darius trusted him the most out of all the ten men.

As the moon's light shone from the window, it reflected on his face making lines of worry that formed on his temples prominent. Darius was pacing back and forth when one of the men he trusted came into his room.

He bowed down in front of him as a form of respect before he started speaking.

"My grace, I know the case of five Nobel men is what's worrying you," the man said.

"Yes, do you have a suggestion for what I may do?" Darius asked, his voice filled with intrigue.

"In my humble opinion, you know better, my king, but I think you must bring them in front of you and ask them yourself. They will dare not to lie to your face," the man said.

Darius nodded approvingly. He then called out for his servants to bring all five of them in front of him.

One by one, all of them were brought to Darius. Their disapproval was not enough not to suspect their involvement.

"Let them stay hungry. Don't give them water to drink. Hold them back from even eating a fly or drinking their swear," he ordered his men.

He was ruthless, leaving the noblemen to be thirsty and hungry. He was not ready to believe that Intraphenes had acted alone, even after seven days of relentless probing. The men did not change their answers. They were innocent. The Nobel men were too few to defend themselves, even against the king. They helped succeed the throne. They knew none of their lives would be spared if Darius even sensed disloyalty. One by one, all of them denied the allegations that were put forth against them. All of them separately had been cleared of the doubts that were against them. They were free to go.

As soon as Darius was pleased that Intaphrenes had acted entirely on his initiative, Intraphenes was arrested along with his children and all his near relations. He was under strong suspicion that he and his family were about to raise a revolt. All the prisoners were then chained as condemned criminals.

Similarly, Itraphenes was wrapped in chains. The clinking of his chains echoed in the palace walls as he walked toward the king, his body filled with scabs. Fresh blood was dripping from the wounds of torment. He looked around at the council that watched him, eagerly waiting to see the sentence. Once a prime example of luxury and power, Intraphenes was now destined and prisoned for everyone to see.

"Intraphenes," the king whispered when he saw him. His face was pale as milk. There was no fear of Intraphenes's face. If there was, he was brave enough to hide it.

"Come ... closer."

Darius' men brought him close. Intrapehens steadied himself but did not want to look weak. He knew the fate that awaited him. He was not going to meet death with a cowardly face. He looked down at Darius to know how abysmal he was.

"What ... ?" He began, his throat clenched. He had been kept without water. His lips were dry as a bone.

"This is my kingdom. Write it with blood on your body if you may ever forget the will and word of King Darius the Great. I do hereby command Intraphenes, the former leader of my army, to be sentenced to death for planning a conspiracy against me and the holy regime of Ahura Mazda until his body begs for release. I, King of Persia, order the severing of his head from his body." Darius had no expression on his face.

"Yes, my king," the men said as they began to take Intraphenes away.

Darius continued to look Intraphenes dead in his eyes as his head was being separated from his body. Darius could almost feel Intraphenes' blood on his lips. There was no one in the entire establishment that would refute this judgment, for disagreeing with the king was worse than treason. The king had made a ceremony about his power for everyone to learn from.

As Intraphenes was leaving, Darius asked a cup filled with blood to be brought for his people, "All of you should witness the blood of Intraphenes and his family." The king said as he was presented to each member of his family one after another. He wanted to shame Intraphenes.

Darius' military campaign started with appointing Intaphrenes as head of his army and seizing back power in Babylon. Later on, having sentenced the rest of the Intaphrenes family to be all put to death, except for his wife, King Darius was moved by the mourning of his wife and allowed her to be rescued from death.

The wife of Intraphenes selected her brother to be spared from the wrath of King Darius, alleging, according to the well-known tale, that she might obtain another husband and other children. However, since her father and mother were dead, she could never have another brother. Darius spared, in addition to her, her eldest child's life, but killed all the other members of the family with Intaphernes. This then was the early end of one of the seven coconspirators.

In the midst of the massacre of Intraphenes and his family, King Darius looked at the lifeless bodies of the people he had slaughtered. Their bodies were decapitated. The glazed ceramic that titivated the surface of Darius' palace once was rubicund with blood. The spattered spoils of flesh did not bother Darius. He walked up to where the beheaded, blood-stained body of Intraphenes rested. The smithereens of his flesh stained the floor. He asked one of his men to come forward. "Hold the head of the traitor who is Intraphenes. Let it be known that I will not be kind to those who conspire against me." His voice echoed off the walls drowning every other noise in the arena.

The king closed his eyes and seemed to relax, but the relief was not for long. As a final point, Darius had thought that he was through with planning strategies against coups. He had thought the display of power and aggression against the Babylonians was enough to send a message across all regions, but he was wrong. All his involvement with the insurgences at Babylon and the distressing facet of Intaphrenes going behind Darius' back, which filled him with unnecessary doubt, he did get distracted. He ignored other aspects of his kingdom. It was upon this time that Darius came to learn about the Scythians. All this chaos and commotion had given birth to yet another revolution. This time, it was amongst the Scythians.

The aroma of war had set itself in the empire of Persia. Everywhere Darius looked, there was a new coup forming against him and his people. The fear of being attacked by other rogues kept him on edge and halted him from living freely. His scheme of expansion looked like a dream to him, but Darius did not give up.

***

The Scythians were nomadic people who controlled the north of the Persian Empire at the Pontic steppes. They did not have much, but they had the influence of extortion. The Scythians were believed to have been of Iranian origin, and they were one of the most skilled horsemen of their time. They spoke a language of the Scythian branch of the Iranian languages.

While Darius was busy with the Babylonian insurgency, Scythians took advantage of this power vacuum and attacked the empire south of the Black Sea. People who were referred to as the Scythians by the Greeks and Saka by the Persians dominated an area that started from the Danube and extended east far beyond the Caspian Sea; Herodotus, yet, the term Scythians was used to referring specifically to those members of this group that lived between the Danube and the Don. As the expansion of the regime began, this region became of particular interest to the Greeks, for it controlled the rivers, but Persia under King Darius' role was not willing to give up even an inch of its power.

The Scythians were not believers of military intimidation; however, they made up their minds to rebel as time evolved.

Scythian Relief at Persepolis

News of this new uprising building midst another part of his regime infuriated him. He was not going to let anyone else take the rule he worked so hard for. He could not trust any man enough to resolve the riot. Darius was prepared to revolt with no minute to spare.

When the news of another rebellion rang across the streets of Persia, Darius was startled. He did not have the support of the crowds in his realm, yet he did have a strong army and loyal men who stood beside him no matter the cause.

The atmosphere of the war was already set, and the Persian Empire had thought of a plan, the only plan that seemed adequate at the time. In the face of Scythian stubbornness and their fixation with going forward with the military offense, Darius was left with no other option but to plan an attack. He did not want these rebellions to become a hurdle in his schemes of expansion.

King Darius was a daring man. No storm could dull the fire that was incinerated inside him. As soon as he came learned of the said invasion, he prepared an expedition into Scythia abounding in men and vast sums flowing into the treasury. The craving to seize them made him hungry to punish the Scyths. They had once in days gone by invaded media, and so begun the quarrel between the two.

Darius spared no cost to verbose this revolt. He ordered his subjects to provide troops and ships to invade Scythia and build a bridge across the Thracian Bosporus. Darius' aura of invincibility reflected the unprecedented scale and speed of his conquests. His overconfidence scared his brother, Artabanos, which was why he tried to convince Darius not to invade Scythia.

Darius had not heard of his brother's plight before today as one of his men came headed toward him at the silence of the night when everyone was asleep to inform the king that his brother was there to see him and awaiting his arrival in the chamber.

By the time Darius entered his chamber, there was no one. He looked around and there he stood at the door. He entered Darius' chamber when he was alone to avoid the risk of conflict.

Artabnos wore a black velvet robe that brushed the floor. His face was filled with lines of strain. "My king, my brother, you are the most knowledgeable. But today, I am here to ask you not to divulge yourself with the war against the Scythians. Your stature is too high and mighty for you to engage with savages like them," Artabanos said.

"Every moment we delay gives them another moment to prepare," Darius said. His voice was oozing with pride.

"We must get the Scythians and see our enemies with our eyes as we take them in hand. I am the protector of this kingdom. I hold the kingdom and all its people in my hand. We should seize the Scythians. This is how we bring balance to the world. Once we have them with us, the others will not dare oppose us. Do not worry, brother," Darius said. He had a taste of rebels once he could not let a little group of thugs disrupt this regime.

All Artabanos could do was warn him against it, but Darius was not too keen on listening. He explained to his brother that he did so not only to uphold Persian interests but also in resistance as he saw it. He called it "the moral balance of the universe."

Artabanos could not argue if he did, it would result in treason and his death, so he bowed their heads and backed away respectfully. Darius was not intrigued by his worries and knew there was no honor in supporting away now.

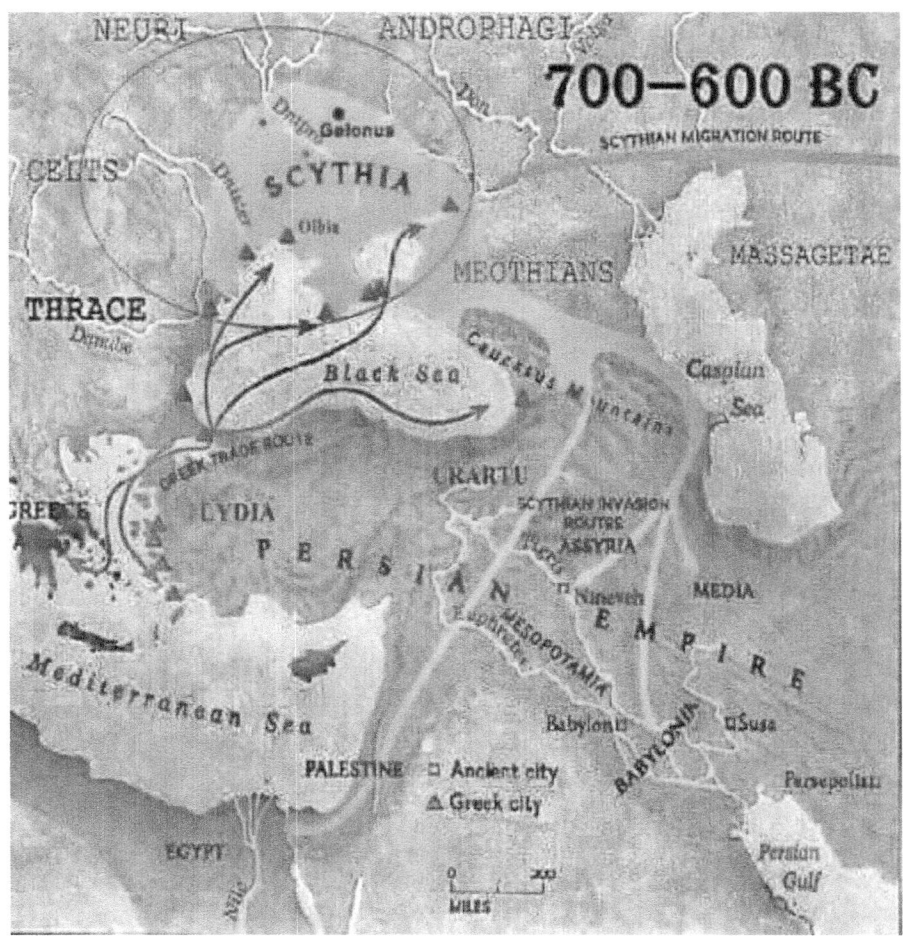

Darius prepared the Persian troops to near Scythians as he could not let them get away with troubling his regime. One day as he was setting his army out for the expedition, he came out to greet all of them and motivated them to march forward with brave hearts. It was a hot day. The sun was shining in all its might when he stood in front of the thousands of men in his army.

"Go and take over whatever land you might see. Kill any life you come across and take for yourself anything you like from the Scythians," Darius commanded as he addressed his army.

However, on Darius' response of attack, the Scythians fled, heading back to their lands north of the Black Sea. He justified his actions to do so because he saw the Scythians as liars and aid to the demons and had felt called upon to pacify them.

Upon seeing their return, Darius did not hold back. He then ordered his troops.

"Go chase them out. I want them to be taken over," Darius wrote in his messages as he sent the envoys to spread his message to every corner the Persian troops were present.

Persian Navy

As Darius and his men crossed the Black sea through Bosphorus Straight using pontoon bridges, the Scythian army was led by a fierce leader named Sarmato.

He was dressed in a robe-like kilt that reached his knees. It was the color of blood. The pleat of the robe was long enough to give him the advantage to hide his weapons. A shoulder-piece was attached to the upper rear section of the kilt to support his backs. He used to hit and run revolutionary tactics against the Persians and was quite famous for being ferocious. The Scythians did not rely on weapons and military strategies but on inventions and exploiting their enemy.

Sarmato had sent a word to the territories that rested from corner to corner near the region. He wanted help and was not afraid to ask for it. He sent out a message to their leaders.

"My fellow liege, battles are not won with men and weapons. They're won with tactic and commitment. The threat of a Persian invasion looms the gates of our barren land. For our acreage to emerge victorious, we need aid. There is nothing better for the people of our lands than to become allies with one another. If we do not join hands, I fear I do not foresee a good future for you and me."

The Scythians and their allies had something Darius and his grand military didn't. They had some land. They could count on the advantage they had given their freedom of movement. They weren't afraid to leave their land to stretch beyond the marks of war. Even though some of their men had taken control of the soil and established permanent settlements around the area, it did not matter. They were all willing to revert to their nomadic ways for the sake of disassembling King Darius' scheme of acquisition. Their skill of mounted archery only abetted them in causing more annihilation. They only had one goal in mind, to shred the Persian territories to pieces.

Sarameto was an adaptable man, unafraid of anything. He used the scorched earth tactics as he geared up and aimed to destroy anything that might be useful to the enemy. Sarameto and his men targeted everything that came in their way: weapons, vehicles, tents, and resources. He harassed the enemy as opposed to facing the Persians in an open battle. Darius sent a message to Sarmato that either stay and fight or surrender.

"Even the bravest leader cannot protect his people against an army like mine. If you want to fight, we will fight with every means we have. If you submit to us, we will let you go. Remember submission is your only option if you want your people to live," Darius warned.

Scythian Archer

The messengers had been dispatched to leave for Sarmato with the king's commands. A man such as Darius was not lightly defied. Sarmato knew that he could not face the mighty Persian army head-on and moved his troops eastward north of the Black sea. The Scythians, reflecting on their situation, perceived that they were not resilient enough by themselves to put up with Darius' army in an open fight. The Scyths were tougher than most. They had heart and bravery, but they lacked wealth and manpower.

King Darius' qualms did not end there. His men were losing control of the area as the days progressed. The extreme policy the Scythians had adopted turned out to be fruitful. But Darius knew he had the manpower he tried to muddle through by mobilizing an army large enough to make a clean sweep of the entire Scythian land. His purpose was clear. He wanted to dispose forever of whatever tedious territory the Scythians had by smoking them out with a battle all across their territory. He was not going to leave any stone unturned. Despite the advice of his generals, he wanted to supply a large army deep in enemy territory. He knew the scorched earth policy of the Scythians could be frustrated by a power that had the resources of Persia if transportation was adequate.

Darius' words twisted in the heart of Scythians like a knife. For a moment, they were at a loss. They could see that defeat awaited them. Saramato could not bring himself to lie to his people about the future of the revolt as they could not fight them on the battlefield.

Scythian Soldier

But he did not want the Scythians to give up. He pledged to his people that they weren't going to go down by being humiliated. They may not have had resources and an army as strong as Darius, but they did have pride. He replied by sending his messenger to Darius.

"We will not stand and fight with Darius until you find the graves of our fathers and try to destroy them. Until then, we could continue our current technique as we have no cities or cultivated lands to lose. This is my answer to the challenge to fight."

The message was not welcoming. It was a warning that was destined for Darius. The Scythians were not scared of them, as they had nothing to lose. Darius hastily ordered a cessation at the banks of Oarus, where he built eight frontier fortresses, spaced at intervals of eight miles. He wanted to hunt them out, but after chasing the Scythians for a month, Darius' army was also suffering losses due to fatigue, privation, and sickness.

With violence increasing each day and men lying dead every minute, the Persians now held a council to decide on the fate of their army and their sanctuary from Scythia. They knew Darius would never say no to the guidance given to him by the Mighty Ahura Mazda. The assembly decided on calling the armed forces back home. They sent out a message that steered him and the army toward safety.

"Ahura Mazda is watching us and wants us to leave."

The news of the counsel reached Darius. He knew this was the smartest move to take at this point. Darius followed the advice of his counsel and agreed to leave. He trusted his guidance to be true. He knew Ahura Mazda would not abandon him and his army easily.

They set out late that afternoon by leaving his sick soldiers and those whose loss would be of least account. With the asses also tied near the camp, Darius marched away. The donkeys were left as their hooves would make a sound and alert the Scythians.

In fear of losing more troops, he halted the march at the banks of the Volga River and headed toward Thrace. He had conquered enough territory of Scythia to force them to respect the Persian forces.

As the last light faded in the Territory of Scythia and the gray day became the black night, Darius asked the Persian army to retreat. He did not want to continue the aggression as he feared more loss of life. He knew the Persian army would stand against him if he lost the war. He made the wise decision to stop when he had the chance.

All the events of Scythia unfolded in front of his eyes. King Darius reflected on his regime. He was certain he was now an expert with warfare and kingdom management. After obtaining his authority over the entire empire, he embarked on a campaign to Egypt, where he defeated the armies of the Pharaoh and secured the lands that Cambyses had conquered while incorporating a large portion of Egypt into the Achaemenid Empire.

"Whatever there is, I must take control over it before it takes over me," Darius said as he continued his series of campaigns.

Behind Darius' throne, many empires were being taken over by the Persian army on his every command, with Darius setting up his kingdom in every part of the world. Guardsmen would wait for his order to take over another kingdom as longswords and weapons hung from their belts.

Darius had kept his promise. He expanded the Persian state to the whole region. The swords of his men were always ready to kill any man or nation that disputed. The need for spreading out his kingdom was a bitter taste in his mouth. He knew better than to tread softly. He must keep his counsel and play the game of expansion until he was firmly established as the one true king of the land.

The others saw Darius as ignorant of the people he was taking over. However, he knew there would be enough time to deal with the succession when all the other regimes were by his side.

"Once the entire region is taken over, the forces will turn, and we will be the only kingdom that rules over them. Our man, our people, and our horse regiment will have nothing to fear from," Darius said as he clicked his teeth together.

As he took over Egypt, he was standing in front of the people. He announced, "Once." His voice echoed in the large auditorium. "Once, you will see our power, my people here lay an entire kingdom in front of you and me, taken by your men. I will not tell you to stay or go. You must make that choice yourself, but live with knowing that Darius and his armed men will take over your region as we already have." His voice fell to a low whisper. "As I have . . ." Darius knew he was destined to be the king of the entire region.

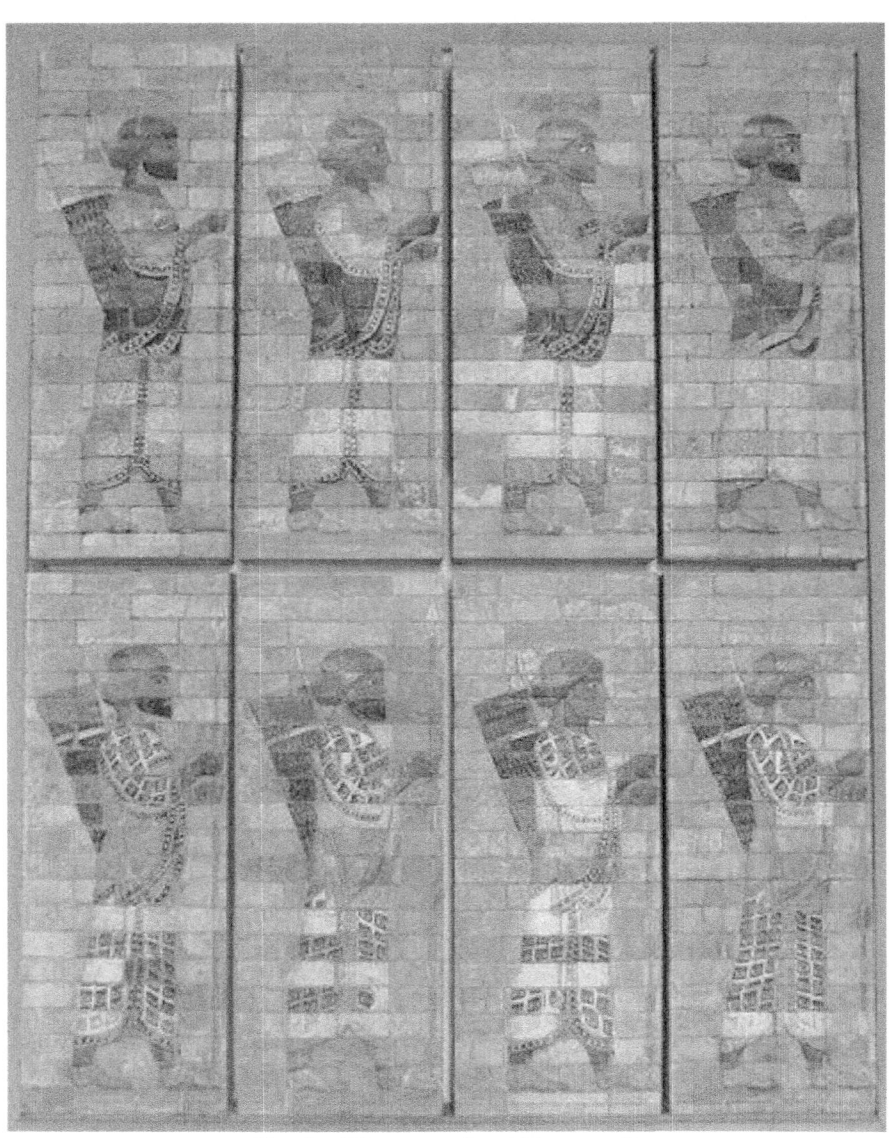

Rank of Immortals at Persepolis

Chapter 9: Greco Persian Wars

Naxos Campaign

Drinks were being poured in large silver and gold goblets, and people were dancing to the loud pounding of drums. The entire Persian Empire was adorned in ornaments. People released loud chants of praises for King Darius the Great and wailed pipes to announce the magnificent victory against Scythia. Outside the empire still laid land that was not under King Darius's control, but there was nothing that stopped the Persian Empire and King Darius the Great.

Achaemenid Wine Cup

An aptitude kindled in the masses of the Persian Empire that endlessly struggled to apprehend land throughout Asia, Europe, Africa, and the seas that came between them.

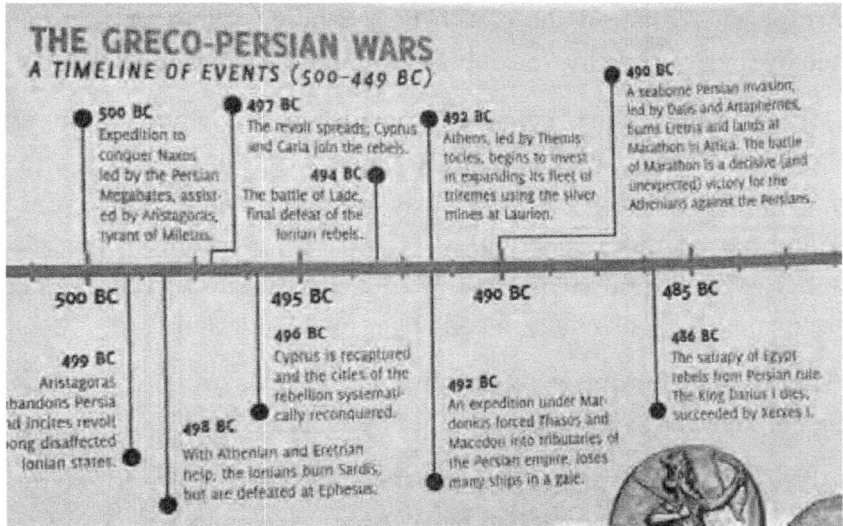

King Darius stood up on a balcony of his castle and proudly gazed upon his kingdom. In his heart, he knew he had to take decisive action against Greece for the Ionian Revolt, which was sponsored and aided by them. He was envisioning an invasion of the entire Greek world, and in his mind, he knew that he had all the resources to rage a war against the Greeks, but he still hesitated. He lacked a grand strategy and got exactly that when Artaphernes paid him a visit amid the silence of the misty night. Darius knew that the deliberations that were going to happen tonight were purportedly clandestine.

Darius was sitting in his chamber wearing a silk robe that was flowing far and wide because of the cool and quiet wind of the night. He was deep in his thought about the imminent future of his kingdom when one of his guards came up to him and told him that Artaphernes, his brother, was here to see him.

"Let him in this second," the king commanded the guard. He wondered if this delightfully unexpected visit was concerning the prospect of the rule or just a sociable visit from a beloved family member.

Artaphernes entered the crater-like chamber. When he saw Darius seated by the grate, he looked at him, stopped, and grew very still.

"My lord, King Darius," came out from his lips in a moment at the sight of the king when he was interrupted by a cackle. Artaphernes, to his horror, looked around to see who was insolent enough to interrupt the king and his brother's meeting, but they were all alone in the vacant chamber. When he saw that it was no one else but his brother, the king, who chortled, his look of alarm and anger turned forgiving.

"I am the king for the world, but to you, I am just a brother," Darius said as he leered at the sight of his brother and embraced him into a hug.

"My king, my brother, I have a message for you from Miletus. It proposes to you and your kingdom to supply vessels and armed personnel to take over Naxos," Artaphernes said as he began to speak about the matter at hand.

"And what does my brother, my general in charge, advise the kingdom regarding this proposal?" Darius asked, shifting in his seat comfortably.

"I suggest we do, my king. The son-in-law of Heistus, Aristagoras the tyrant of Miletus, has taken charge of the fleet himself, and the disposition is well-versed for us to follow through," Artaphernes said as he continued to look down at his feet.

"I understand, but this man you speak of, Aristagoras, seems to have been quite friendless. I'm yet to know anything about him," King Darius said carefully. His voice was cracking as if he was parched, or perhaps the burden of deep thought may have withered his throat.

"My king, if I've given offense, forgive me, but you might find comfort in knowing that he came to me in the flesh to bring this offer forward, but you know better. His proposal, in my humble opinion, is in our best interest. After all, we want to expand over to the Greek lateral," Artaphernes explained.

Somewhere in 499 B.C.E., Aristagoras, the cruel and oppressive ruler of Miletus, approached the satrap, Artaphernes, with a proposition to sponsor a campaign to conquer Naxos, a Greek island in the South Aegean. At first, Artaphernes was reluctant to the proposition, but eventually, he decided to consider his scheme. Aristagoras knew his relationship with King Darius was not in account to be presenting such propositions directly before him, so he convinced Artaphernes. He knew the king trusted him. On the other hand, the concern of taking over 200 Persian ships was risky, especially when he was not sure of the consequences.

King Darius wondered if Artaphernes' confidence in this strategy was enough to give him the fleet. "Naxos is Greek territory, and I do sense that the conclave against the Persian realm is on the verge of building there. We must act fast before it turns into another rebellion," Darius spoke. Once he gave his due consideration to the proposal in front of him, the king spoke in all his command.

The final verdict from Darius comforted Artaphernes. He knew this was his way of giving authorization. The only way to compose this was to send the fleet to Greece. On the other hand, Kind Darius wondered if Artaphernes' confidence was enough to place Aristagoras in charge of the Persian fleet.

Seal of Darius The Great

The king dismantled his comfort and stood up from his throne. He raised another concern. He told Artaphernes that in order for his heart to find peace, he must send someone he trusted to accompany Aristagoras in Naxos. He asked his brother if he had any suggestions. At this point, Artaphernes did not want to take any responsibility. Therefore, he maintained his silence and articulated to the kind that he had no one in his mind. The king decided to take the matters into his own hand and summoned Megabates.

Megabates was a military leader in King Darius' army. He was also the cousin of Darius and his brother Artaphernes. The announcement of bringing Megabates did not alarm Artaphernes. After all, he was a blood relative. Moreover, all Artaphernes could do ahead of the king's decision was nod swiftly and sway past him in his respect.

***

138

Megabates was sound asleep, almost benumbed when he was called in the chamber of King Darius. He hurriedly got dressed and ran from across the largely deserted land to meet the king, who had explicitly asked him to be fetched.

The wait for Megabates seemed long. The king and his brother were on their third glass of wine before the guard entered the chamber escorting the sought-after Megabates. He bowed slightly as he made his way inside, where the two brothers were standing. Megabates knew his face was flushed, but in darkness, King Darius could not tell. Megabates sensed the presence of no one else but the two brothers – his cousins.

There was nothing about the arrangement that led him to believe why this midnight call was a matter of grave urgency. He was too somnolent to understand the crux of the matter. After all, he had just been woken up from deep sleep, He wasn't even aware of the theme of the discussion that the two brothers were having, but Megabates knew better than to condemn the king's resolution for him in the middle of the night.

The kind ordered Megabates to sail to Miletus the next morning and fight Naxos with Aristagoras. His words struck him as a surprise. He had many questions in his mind, but he knew the king did not need his agreement. He was aware of the fact that King Darius decided to send someone he trusted, someone that shared the same blood as him, for blood is thicker than water, or so he had thought. He took this very emotionally. With that, the night's discussion clinched.

No windstorm could frighten the great king, and even though a proposal of an excursion to Naxos did satisfy the king, he was wiser than to take someone's word for it. He had learned to be careful, especially after the incident with Intaphernes.

The next morning, Darius was standing on top of a hill looking upon the fleet of ships that were lined all ready for the voyage. As the sun's initial rays touched the earth, Megabates, with his fleet of 200 ships, headed for Miletus.

As old and experienced as he was, Megabates had never seen a fleet of ships half so gargantuan and grandeur like the one prepared for Aristagoras. As the journey proceeded, he leaned against the barricade of the ship he commanded, looking beyond the mighty blue sea. The sea was crashing beneath him, and the tiny droplets from the waves were almost touching his fingers. Megabates felt the sense of tranquility overtake him, but perhaps, it was the calm one feels before a storm.

The fleet followed its course and sailed for Chios, where the ships anchored in preparation for the attack on Naxos, and that's where the two men, Aristagoras and Megabates, met.

Aristagoras was the prime force of the plan, whereas Megabates was the man reserved in charge of the fleet by King Darius himself. The animosity between the two was inevitable. At their first glimpse, both men had nothing but abhorrence for each other. After a few hours of darkness amid their stay, the convoy of large ships began to sail for Naxos.

Megabates was wary of Aristagoras. He suspected of some foul play amongst the men of his own fleet. He didn't sleep the night and instead decided to watch over the men. He learned that the sentries, who were given the orders of keeping watch over the ship, had not been set on board on one of the ships. Megabates was fuming with anger. He knew this was a stint when his men would have woken him, no matter the hour, to have him there to give his guidance as soon as they learned of the error, yet they didn't. He knew he had to take action, for combat ships were not the place for friendly men.

Fuming with rage, Megabates commanded his troops to fetch the skipper of the ship, Scylax. Megabates confronted him and ordered his men to pull him through the oar-hole of the ship as punishment.

Meanwhile, some men informed Aristagoras about the unbridged trial of the captain. He stormed out of his cabin and saw Scylax begging for his life. It filled him with rage.

"It seems like you have forgotten your place, Megabates," Aristagoras exclaimed. "You're no king to edict punishment."

Megabates was outraged. He felt humiliated by Aristagoras. He could only think of one thing that would disgrace Aristagoras, and that was warning the Naxos of his attack.

The plan was set, and it was a clever one. Megabates retaliated by sending word to Naxos in the darkness of the night when no prying eyes would catch the malevolent plan of his disloyalty. He warned the Naxians that they were about to be attacked. The Naxians, without one iota of doubt in his missive, took this as an opportunity to secure their walls.

While the Naxians prepared for a siege, just a few miles away was Aristagoras' fleet, completely unaware of the warning as they sailed for the island. When the convoy finally arrived, the guardsmen outside the territory knew the fleet by sight. They had been expecting them. The Persians, upon their arrival, found Naxos so well defended. They could not take it and lay siege.

Artwork by Richard Hook

The Persians initiated assaulting the city but botched and lost hundreds of men. Despite possessing only 8,000 hoplites and 4,000 zyphus for hand-in-hand combat against 20,000 Persians, each carrying a bow, a spear, a sword or ax, and a wicker shield, the Naxians didn't surrender to their fates and fought valiantly. Naxians wisely utilized the time they were given and secured the walls of their city. They brought all the rations inside their walls, so people would have an ample amount of food during the ensuing siege.

As the barricade dragged on for four months, the Persians kept dwindling every passing day. While the Naxians were well supplied behind their walls, the ephemeral force steadily ran out of supplies and food. The Persians looked feeble and lacked a clear strategy.

Persian Navy

The huge fleet of ships and the thousands of Darius' men were stuck behind the well-protected walls of the city. With no end in sight, Aristagoras was forced to turn the ships around for Miletus. He knew he had to leave. The first Persian invasion against the Greeks failed.

However, the secret of treachery laid safe with Megabates. Not a single word reached Darius. He was oblivious that it was Megabates, his own cousin, who betrayed his empire for petty revenge. Aristagoras' original plan had completely failed. He had failed to fulfill his promise. The most significant part was he had been defeated. He now had to deliver this news to Artraphernes, who would, of course, inform Darius.

Aristagoras feared he would be stripped of his title, or worse, be exiled or even executed. He had to think of a way out to extricate himself. Aristagoras himself regretted his decision. Shuffling and walloping along the pathway to Miletus, Aristagoras thought, and he thought hard. "How will I be able to get out of this?" was the only thing the general could think of.

It was a troubling grievance, deeply felt, and never more so than now. Here General Aristagoras was on his way back to Miletus with the news of defeat when a messenger arrived from Histiaeus, his uncle, at Susa. There he was standing in front of Aristagoras, hiding from the eyes of intrigue that followed him, and when the two of them were safe and alone in a room, he told Aristagoras the reason for his advent. His throat clenched before he spoke. He was afraid, but he had to speak.

"I am a slave of your uncle. I have been sent for your aid. There is a message contained by me that ought not to be read by someone else. Even I do not know what the message is. It is only for your eyes to see," the man said courteously.

Aristagoras stopped midway and pressed his lips together to think. The objective of this man's excursion was unknown. He had to discern his message to know better. But in his heart, he recognized that whatever this may be was sent for help.

Histiaeus was vigilant and had strictly warned Aristagoras that his message should only be read by Aristagoras. He had planned precisely for that. He shaved the head of one of his slaves. When there was no more hair on his head, he tattooed the message for his nephew on the man's scalp with ink. When the slave's hair finally grew back, he sent him on his mission.

The message incited Aristagoras to start an uprising in Miletus. The envoy turned around and bowed his head for Aristagoras to read. Histiaeus wrote in his message, "I must add my voice to yours. Root a rebellion, for you have the right people for it and bear in mind that not only will it help you, my dear nephew, but it will also relieve me."

Aristagoras was aware that his uncle, Histiaeus, was sick of being confined in Susa. He knew a man like his uncle would not give false hope. Aristagoras read the message narrow-eyed and went into deep thought. Had he lived so long, only to betray the people who trusted him, for the sake of his own life?

"It is a dreadful thing to do, yet I know it must be done," Aristagoras spoke softly.

Chapter 10: The Ionian Revolt

The fear in Aristagoras' heart overtook his passion for loyalty. He thought about fleeing, but he was aware of King Darius' wrath. If even one word reached his ear about Aristagoras' absconding, he would command his army of hundreds of thousands to hunt him alive. Aristagoras wanted to remain true to the man who had helped him, yet the judgment was hard.

What would a man choose between his life and loyalty?

"I can't face the king when I stand defeated, nor can I bring a revolution without an army!" Aristagoras was deep in his thoughts, for no one could hear him. He sensed the wavering fear in his heart, growing with every fleeting moment. He struggled to make a decision that would keep him alive. The only thing he could think of was to inflame another uprising. He had to make a decision and he had to make it now. He had no moment to lose, for the king awaited his return. After due reflection, he decided it was best for him to incite a rebellion. He chose his life above allegiance.

Aristagoras, the extant ruler of the Ionian city of Miletus, had discerned that his people would support him. All he had wanted for as long as he could remember was power and glory, but now, he was going face to face with death. Aristagoras was aware that the time to incite such a deed must be precise. The Persians were without a fleet of two hundred ships, for Aristagoras had taken charge of them to make his journey to Naxos. He sensed a weakness within the army of King Darius – the man he had now decided to make his enemy. He sent word to his people. It was an open call to rebel against the Persian empire. He was aware of the risk that the message carried as it was an invitation to war.

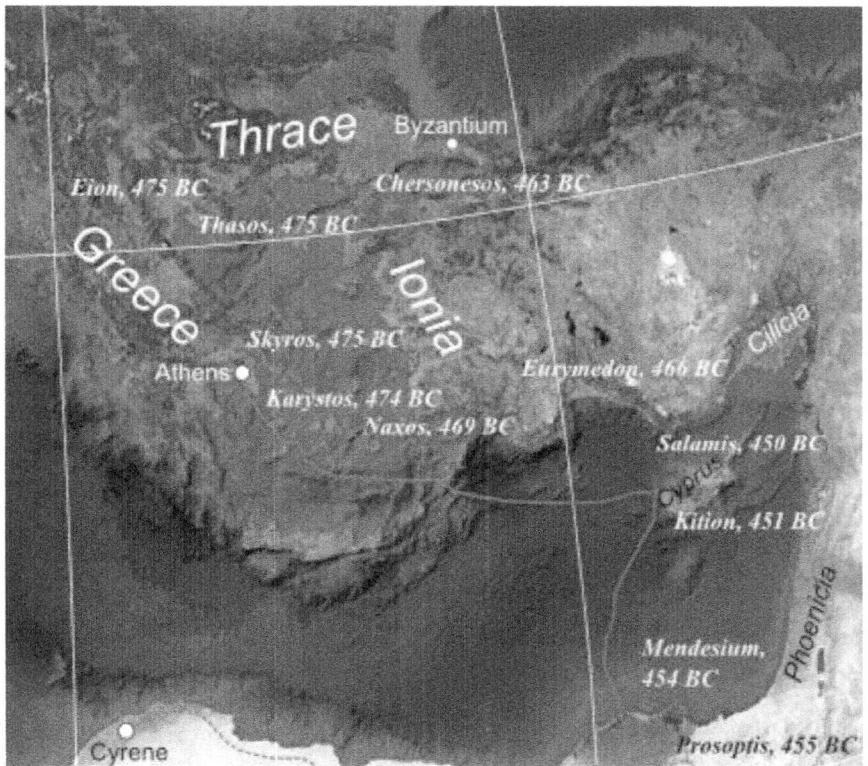

Ionia

Aristagoras chose to incite the whole of Ionia into rebellion against the Persian Empire. He acquiescently declared his revolt against Darius, abandoned his title, declared Darius as a tyrant, and declared Miletus a democracy. He turned toward his people and conveyed his message of acquiescence.

"You have more right to make pronouncements about your land than I do. I hereby give up the power that was bequeathed upon me by Darius and give back the power to you, The People of this Great Land. We cannot achieve sovereignty if we stay with Persia. If we respect our land, we must rise."

His speech had done precisely what he hoped. It lit a spirit of mutiny in the hearts of the Ionian people. Aristagoras distinguished that to make the Ionian support him. He had to renounce the authority granted to him by King Darius.

Once the wind of his allegiance shifted and the announcement of his resolution reached across lands, Aristagoras invigorated all the other Ionians to remove their leaders. The sound of intense shouts and screams echoed in city streets. The people of Ionia had chosen to take over their cities. The retort was filled with force; many cities in the area protested and banished their Persian rulers. High, mighty, and strong men of the acreage all stood in support of Aristagoras. His plan looked like it was working.

Aristagoras' true colors were finally out in the open, and he was growing braver with every stroke of his strategy. The dagger of his insurgence was not yet set. He knew that with King Darius' prestige on the line, it would not be long until he retaliated.

Aristagoras knew behind the walls of his insignificant domain that an enormous army awaited him. If he was not quick, all his planning would end in chaos. He quickly traveled to Sparta and appealed to King Cleomenes for aid. He used the prisoner of wars from the cities and sent men to capture all the Greek tyrants present in the army and handed them over to their respective cities to gain their cooperation.

All the same, it was a mistake to think that asking for Spartan patronage would be this easy. Aristagoras' path to glory was one filled with thorns, for when the Spartan leader learned of the distance his army would have to travel to support the Ionians, he declined the request for aid. The Spartans knew the battle was a death sentence. They knew if they stepped in this battle, it would be for a losing cause.

Aristagoras did not see this coming. The shattering noise of his broken dreams disrupted his vision. He had hoped it would be easy to convince King Cleomenes. The malaise of his decline was the first step in the great conflict between Persia and Greece.

Apprehensive of the Persian emperor's punishment, Aristagoras and his people were desperate for support. Next, they went to Athens for help. The Athenians, fearing an inevitable attack by the Persians, decided to support Aristagoras and sent twenty (20) triremes, an oar-driven warship, along with five from Eretria. The Athenians were powerful, yet they were not as skilled at war and conflict as the Spartans. Nonetheless, Aristagoras's desperation for military power was on the rise. He could not risk his plot being unsuccessful.

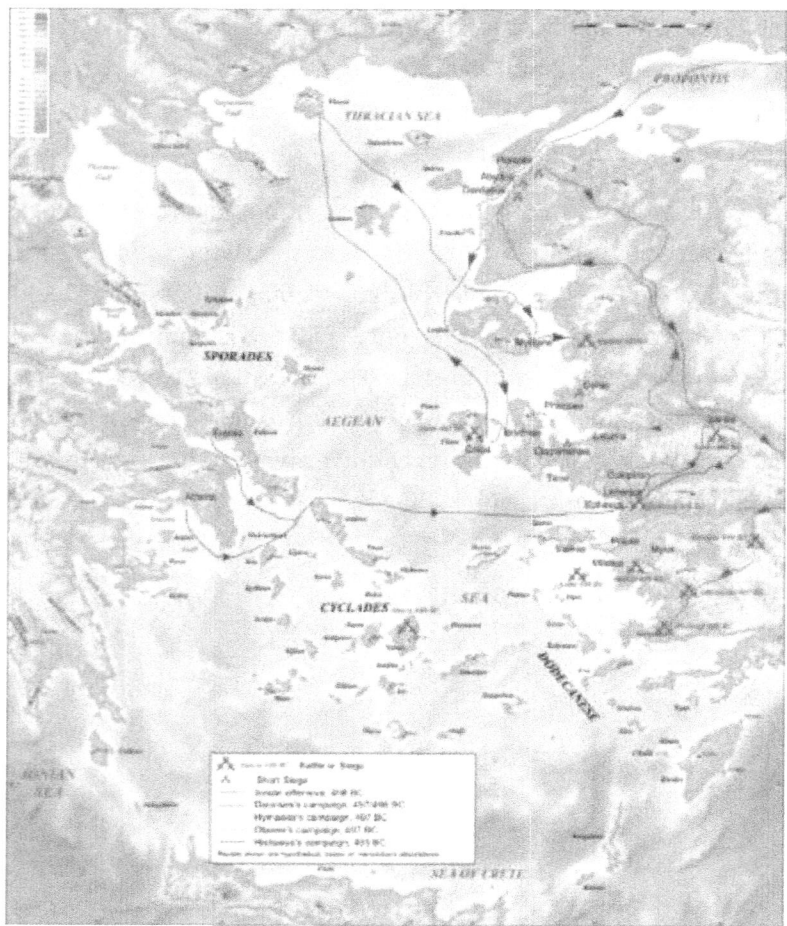

The plan was simple. The Ionian fleet, bolstered by Athenian and Eritrean ships, would sail to Ephesus, the ancient Greek city on the coast of Ionia, and rage war on the Persians.

The ships that would prove to be the beginning of the evil for the Greeks were chained at the port of Coressus, and the soldiers followed the river Cayster to Sardis. It was a vital city for the Persians and the Greeks to control.

Their war strategy was to invade the lands in silence, for the Persians did not know of their adventure yet. The Allied Greek forces marched into the city, where they met little resistance, for King Darius was still oblivious to Aristagoras' schemes.

Breaking the agreement of loyalty was not something the King of Persia would take lightly. As soon as the news reached King Darius of Aristagoras' treachery, he rose in anger.

"How dare the man who I trusted with my army betray me?" There was not a hair on his body that was not all set to take revenge.

King Darius wanted to show his fury and power. His oath of vengeance was set, and he wanted the people of Persia to know that in the face of this small lapse of judgment, he was still in control of the vast Persian empire. He called onto the only man he could trust, Artaphernes, for no one except his brother was worthy of taking care of the king's commands.

As the Ionian army marched deeper into the city, they finally came across Artaphernes, the man who was defending the citadel. They had not expected him to be there. Artaphernes, on knowledge of the Great King Darius, was leading his army on the verge of a heroic clash. Each one of King Darius's men was equipped with double the armor and weapon than the Ionians. If they wanted to get access to the city, they would have to sacrifice their lives, for danger was all around them.

More and more Ionian men perished to the ground, and the fear that smashed onto their faces was palpable. Not able to capture the citadel, the Ionians set the city ablaze and retreated to Ephesus. The citadel was left in flames, yet it remained imperishable.

The dawn of Darius' men was nigh. Aristagoras could sense something ruthless and wicked headed for him. Not too far away from the citadel, in their land, the Persian army waited for orders to attack and finish the Ionian army. Countless men and supplies appeared before them. The king's command of a bloodbath was inevitable, and before long, the Persian troops began pouring in. There was a constant stream of men, ordnances, and large fleets of equipped recruits assembling in the area. The place for the battle was set. They were only waiting for the order to attack.

Under the atmosphere of the battle, the message carrying the order traveled to the Persian army. It was the long-awaited order to rouse vehemence. In due time, the mayhem started. Persian troops in the area met the Greeks at Ephesus and massacred most of them. The remaining Ionians scattered to the surrounding cities. Hundreds and thousands of men slashed each other like animals, and with time, the air was screaming with the sound of screams.

The sun dyed the horizon bloody-red at Ephesus. The battlefield was covered with the blood and flesh of the dead. Persians did not leave any man alive. The clanking of the swords boomed everywhere, corpses laid on the paths of the city, and the flies swarmed in drinking the blood of the dead. There was no mercy left for anyone.

Persians Battling Greeks

Despite the great setback of losing so many men, Aristagoras continued his fight against Persia. He encouraged more revolts in Western Asia Minor, Thrace, and Cyprus. It was a sign that Aristagoras knew very well. The war was now at its peak. He sent part of his fleet to aid the Cyprians, but the Persians thoroughly defeated the Cyprian army. Aristagoras had no strategy left to confront the Persian army now. Every one of his tactics had started to fail.

King Darius had decided to attack Caria, a city with close ties to Miletus, Aristagoras's city. If he wanted to humiliate Aristagoras in front of his people, this was the only way to do it.

However, through some ploy, the Carians learned of this plan. They ambushed the Persian army at night and massacred it. The Persian Army lost some of its most prominent leaders. Even though their deaths were a great forfeiture, Persia could not stop now. Not when the reputation of their Great King was at stake. They diligently continued to siege the Ionian cities.

The uncertainty of the situation was hovering over Aristagoras like a flock of vultures with hungry unfriendly eyes. Seeing his upheaval collapse and fearing for his life, Aristagoras fled to Mycrinus. Relentless horror loomed in Aristagoras' mind. If the king caught him, he would be dead in a heartbeat. He gave command of Miletus over to Pythagoras, a mathematician and a non-combatant.

Aristagoras, frustrated with his failed rebellion, attacked the Thracians, who dominated most of the area. Everywhere Aristagoras and his army looked, they were met with resilient carnage and butchery. It was only a matter of time when he and his army were cut off and destroyed. Most of his men were dead. The haunting sounds of their screams did not leave Aristagoras for a moment.

After Aristagoras left Miletus, the Persian fleet sailed to Lade and destroyed the Greek fleet defending the city. King Darius and his army captured Miletus and emerged victorious. After the city-state fell, the revolts in Ionia crumbled due to a lack of leadership.

Nevertheless, this was not the end that the Greeks saw of King Darius' wrath. The riot was going to have many lasting effects. Across the field, the Ionian ignorance ended, and they had been defeated. However, Darius' anger for Athens only grew. He knew this war only happened because of the aid they provided to the Ionians. He could not be content knowing that the Greeks were out there, free to cause another uprising. It gave the king the spur to invade Greece. The rebellion had clearly shown that the empire he had so carefully built and organized was susceptible to attacks from the western frontier.

King Darius' mind was wrapped with the thoughts of punishing Greeks. He knew the time had come when Athens must be conquered.

Chapter 11: Greek Invasion

When the Persian army returned from Ionia, the Mighty King was fuming with anger. The Persian army had defeated the rebels, yet the sound of errant mutinies and uprising still echoed in Darius' mind. Even the slightest sight of the Greeks disgusted him. Darius wondered if there would be a day in his empire where he would be able to rule without any nuisance. The king wanted to punish the Greeks.

At his command lay the powerful Persian army and navy that were well trained and equipped with the best arrows, shields, and ships. Just one command from King Darius was enough to make them sacrifice their life for Persia. For King Darius, it was the right time to invade Greece.

Greece

The voices that surrounded him in his council all wailed and conversed. There was a sense of urgency seen in the convention. The Persian noblemen that filled the room knew what was about to come.

They only awaited the judgment from their leader. The great King sat on his throne, his long hair and beard now mostly gray, his green eyes wide open, motionless, and silent, still listening to the numerous voices that filled the room. He may have been quiet, but his mind was not. He had already thought of the perfect revenge – an invasion of Greece.

Persia's declaration of war was just a few moments away. With his eyes scanning the room, Darius turned pensively to the council of men that sat before him. "Those Athenians!" He paused for a moment. The room's walls were filled with hollers and curses at the mention of the Athenians. "We need to teach them a lesson. Those bastards deserve no mercy." Every corner of the room was now shouting in anger.

"Let the king speak!" A loud commanding voice erupted from the midst of the chaos and screams. It was Darius' son-in-law Mardonius.

"My Lord, I pay my apologies for this horror show of impudence. Please carry on with what you were saying." Mardonius turned toward the king and conversed with him directly. All eyes followed the man that stood there. There was so much power in his voice that the room fell silent in a heartbeat.

King Darius looked at Mardonius. He began to speak once more. "You are a brave man, Mardonius, a great commander, a great military man, and someone I can trust."

"I want you to honor this kingdom with the Achaemenian sword." King Darius picked up the magnificent sword resting on his side. The broad golden metal laid cold beside him. He picked it up and walked toward Mardonius.

It was a gesture of loyalty and trust. The king wanted to assure Mardonius that he had the complete faith of the Persian Empire. The looming responsibility weighed on Mardonius' shoulder. He knew it was a tough ask. The last man who was given this charge was slashed in front of his eyes. It was Mardonius' duty to the kingdom that he accepted the symbol.

"My king, I hope I don't fail you and Persia." Mardonius bowed to King Darius. He weighed the ice-cold steel in his hand. It was agreed. Mardonius was going to invade Greece.

Achaemenid Sword

Without a word more, King Darius walked back to retake his seat at the throne. The loud cheers of felicitations annexed the king's mind. He would only be at ease once the Athenians were defeated. He picked up the noise ringing in the room. "May the Athenians ache and grieve." The men cheered loudly. They raised their swords high in the air, anticipating war and destruction.

The conflict stood waiting in the wings. "Let's hope this is our last time at war." A voice whispered in the king's ear. That is what the king hoped for. He wanted to watch Greece be punished. He was not prepared to let more of his men die.

***

Thousands of men prepared to fight for Persia. Everyone was ready and willing to go. They only waited for one thing; the king's command to leave. In due time, the order came ringing through the halls of the Perspolis Palace. An expeditionary force, to be commanded by King Darius' handpicked man, Mardonius, was assembled. It consisted of a fleet of armed ships and a land army.

King Darius had only one wish in his mind. He wanted Athens to suffer just as much as Ionia had. However, King Darius' ultimate intention was to castigate and humiliate Athens. The men who surrounded the king suggested thinking wisely. The expedition also aimed to subdue as many of the Greek cities as possible.

Departing from the land of Cilicia, Mardonius sent the army to march to the Hellespont. This was a challenging task, and Cilicia was the only probable land route to Athens. Nevertheless, Mardonius did not want to give the responsibility of his armada to another general. He had a strategy at play for Ionia, and he only trusted himself to implement it. He decided to move with the fleet. Mardonius sailed around the coast of Asia Minor to

Ionia, where he spent his time obliterating the cruelties that ruled Ionian cities.

He wanted the people of Ionia to have the power to choose their leaders. As luck would have it, the Ionians would go back to when obtaining consensuses had been a critical factor in the Ionian Revolt. Mardonius pledged to replace the cruel tyrannies that overtook their land with democracies.

Mardonius' establishment of democracy in Ionia was all just part of the grand strategy. He had hoped to calm Ionia with this move. In return, the Ionians would have no choice but to agree and protect the western borders of Persia. Mardonius' strategy was quite effective as he advanced toward Hellespont and then onto Athens and Eretria.

The fleet continued to Hellespont, and when all was ready, it shipped the land forces across to Europe. Fear was beginning to clutch the Athenians' hearts once the mighty Persian army marched through Thrace, subjugating it for the second time.

Without pause or hesitation, Mardonius and his army were soaring through the fallen bodies of their enemies. Each annexation was harsher than their last one. Mardonius had a clear strategy and did not let his vision stray. The king himself bestowed him with this task. He would stop at no cost. Upon reaching Macedon, the Persians conquered it and incorporated it as part of the Empire. They had been vassals of Persia for centuries. Their authority and influence were wide-ranging, but for the first time, Macedon was run by a Persian governor.

Painting of Darius on a Greek Vase

***

Meanwhile, the fleet crossed Thasos, resulting in the Thasians submitting to the Persians. The fleet then curved with the coastline as far as their eyes could soar before endeavoring to conquer the cliff of Mount Athos. The ships traveled the waves in serenity until it was face to face with a violent storm.

It was the Persian navy's bad luck that they were caught in a fierce storm. It resounded fear in the hearts of the men that were on board. Monstrous lightning lit the heavens and the skies and declared itself as the conqueror of their armada. Rain pelted down from the sky like a well-orchestrated strategy against the Persians. The wind ran in their direction as if it chased and drove them against the coastline of Athos. The waves from the sea thrashed the ships. They rocked them back and forth, and it took only a moment for the glorious sky to wreck 300 ships. Bit by bit, the vicious gale claimed the lives of Persian men. The deck that was once full of men with bravery in their hearts and lives in their bodies laid dead at sea.

***

Mardonius and his men decided to take shelter in Thasos. For they thought, if they were to fight the army of Greeks, they had to pick up supplies and more troops, but they were not aware of the plan that awaited them.

The soldiers who awaited Mardonius and his men had now started to gain a thrust in the fleet's destruction. Poseidon had already helped the Greeks by wiping more than half of King Darius' Navy. Hundreds and thousands of Greek men rushed forward to plan an attack on the Persian fleet. The Greeks knew the Persians were vulnerable. In their eyes, Darius' army was now scarce. The Thracian army assumed that Persians' lingering men would not make a strong stand, or so they had thought.

In the light of losing men, the Thracians planned an attack in the murkiness of the night. They efficaciously planned a night raid against the

Persian camp. As they waited to go out and kill them all, they were confident they would emerge victorious.

Persian Soldier

Once every cradle of light died, the Territorial Army realized that it was time to attack the camp. The land was dark and quiet. All the men were asleep. The Thracian army was armored, equipped, and ready. King Darius' worst dream was about to come true. His men were about to be attacked. There were many men settling just on the outskirts of where Mardonius and his men rested. Nobody knew the secrets that the Greek army was hiding in the silence of the night.

There was no sign of an intrusion, but the Persian army's fate had already been written. Then the army finally entered. Mardonius and his men had never seen such a treacherous sight. Only a coward attacks at night, they thought, but now the stage was set. The distance was not great, and the men of Therasia were now steadily marching toward them. Spears flew in the air and killed many soldiers.

Mardonius rose with anger and ordered the resting men to prepare themselves for a clash. There was no time left to prepare. He jumped onto his horse and announced to his men to rise. Some had armors and some had helmets, but every one of them was now ready. Mardonius knew they were numerically inferior, but they equipped themselves with armor and rode on their horses' backs, supporting arrows and swords in their hands.

Mardonius the Commander

In the field where the Persian men rested for sleep, now lay dead, lifeless bodies of the Persians and Greeks. Hours and hours passed. There were meat and bones scattered as far as one's eyesight could see. The armed forces entered the land, killing many of the Persians. As the men fought one another, a spear lashed into Mardonius' arm. He was in awful pain. He had been wounded. He had cuts on his hands and knees. He was bleeding badly, but he fought the agony that his injuries were causing him and marched forward. He did not have the time to stop. Mardonius could not. The Thracian army had to be stopped, and the response was vicious.

In the face of his injury, Mardonius did not let it hold him down. Both armies were brimming in a tangle of corpses. He led his army of men that were on foot and horseback into battle. He wasn't going to surrender. His ego would not let him do that. Mardonius did not care about his mortality, but the man that served beside him would not submit to the wrath of the Greeks.

Persians Battling Greeks

Mardonius was proud. The army he was leading was proud and willful and would not let the blood of their lost men go in vain. It was nearly sunrise, but the clash was far from over. Persians fought their way forward and defended the honor of their land bravely. More and more soldiers were dying on both sides. The sound of swinging swords echoed in the darkness of the night.

For the Persians, the legacy that they were carrying with them was paramount. It would have been a much different voyage if their fleet of ships from the islands had not been destroyed, but as the Persians marched into battle, they weren't going to go down without a fight. Even with an ominously smaller army, Mardonius made sure that the Greeks were defeated and subjugated. He was a man of honor and strong willpower. He precisely did what he promised King Darius. He was not going to disappoint his king. Mardonius looked around. The enemy was decisively defeated, but at that moment, he felt his heart at peace. There was now complete control of the battle by Persians.

Achaemenid Flag

Mardonius just had one more thing left to do. He went back to retrieve the broken pieces of the men who died at sea. Then he could lead his army back to his soil. He knew it was time for him to return to the Great King with good news.

For Mardonius, his crusade had ended gloriously. The land approaching Greece had been secured, and the Greeks were undoubtedly made aware of Darius' intentions. The might of King Darius rang in the halls of the newly seized Greek territory.

Mardonius was commanding the army in a battle in Thrace. While Mardonius was wounded in the battle, he was victorious, conquering Thrace and incorporating it back into the empire. Nevertheless, the loss of the fleet meant that he had to retreat into Asia Minor.

***

The moment Mardonius stepped back in the chamber of the king, he knew the judgment that awaited him. He was relieved of his command by Darius, who had his eyes on someone else for the moment he returned.

King Darius did not want a man who led his flotilla into disaster to take care of Greece's next siege. Despite his proof of loyalty, King Darius thought the forfeiture of his men was dishonorable. He was not convinced that Mardonius could take care of such an essential task. He looked at Mardonius, who had now returned home, disenchanted and injured. He was in great pain, but he had to see the king. Mardonius had hoped that the king would be happy with the sacrifices he made for the Empire. However, a shock awaited his arrival.

The king addressed him directly, "Mardonius, your grievance is my shame. The loss of my men is the death of Persians. They're all part of the battle, yet it's just another reminder of my failure."

Mardonius stood there, absorbing not every word the king said to him. It was rare to relieve men like him so soon. He wanted to serve the King of Persia, but he ventured no further word. Mardonius was a man of wrath and anger, much like Darius. It was expected of him to throw a fit, but he controlled his anger.

Instead, to everyone's shock, Mardonius kneeled. He obeyed the king's command, but he knew he had a greater purpose here. He did not dare and say a word. Mardonius' work in the provision of his land would not come to a halt.

Darius sent ambassadors to all Greek cities to claim full submission in light of the recent Persian victory. He wanted all the Greek cities to submit to the rule of the one true Persian king.

In the newly captured territory, Persian men raised their swords high. All eyes in the land turned to King Darius the Great. They had now taken all the land they could under their wing. Nevertheless, another shock awaited the King, for there were exceptions – Athens and Sparta, which had executed Darius' respective ambassadors.

For Darius, the battle had not yet ended. These actions signaled Athens' unrelenting insolence to the king's mighty rule. The Great King was not happy about it. Affronts and insults like this would only result in death. The king would accept nothing less. The Gods had allowed the Athenians to rebel against him into the conflict. He wanted to arrange their destruction now, for the Persian Empire could not wait for another mêlée.

King Darius had seen enough agitations to know that he had to act fast. He swore to burn down Athens and Eretria. Darius had his bow brought to him and then shot an arrow "upward toward heaven," saying in his loud and proud voice: "Ahura Mazda, that it may be granted to me to take vengeance upon the Athenians!" He was raging with anger. He wanted to drag the blood out of their bodies until they were pale and blue.

The disapproval of these territories infuriated him. For the king, it was nothing short of an insult. King Darius burst into his throne room and indicted one of his servants to say, "Master, remember the Athenians," three times before he sat down to eat dinner each day. The king did not want to forget what his resolution was. He had sworn to make the Athenians pay for this gross malfeasance.

Chapter 12: Marathon

Darius knew he had to respond to Athenians and Spartans executing his ambassadors. He sent a naval task force under Datis and Artaphernes, his two loyal generals, across the Aegean Sea to subjugate the Cyclades. He wanted the two generals to make punishing attacks on Athens and Eretria.

The two generals in charge of King Darius' army and navy chose the early spring as the best to enter the territory. There was no time to waste. After a successful campaign in Aegean, they defeated Euboea in mid-summer.

The Persians then proceeded to besiege and capture Eretria, the land that did not accept King Darius as their one true King. The Persians attacked them with great bravery and velour in their hearts. The military thought a special contest awaited their arrival there, but they took over the Eretria land without difficulty. The attack had come to a halt much sooner than they had expected. The Persian force then sailed for Attica, landing in the bay near the town of Marathon. Finally, this was the place where the two armies would meet.

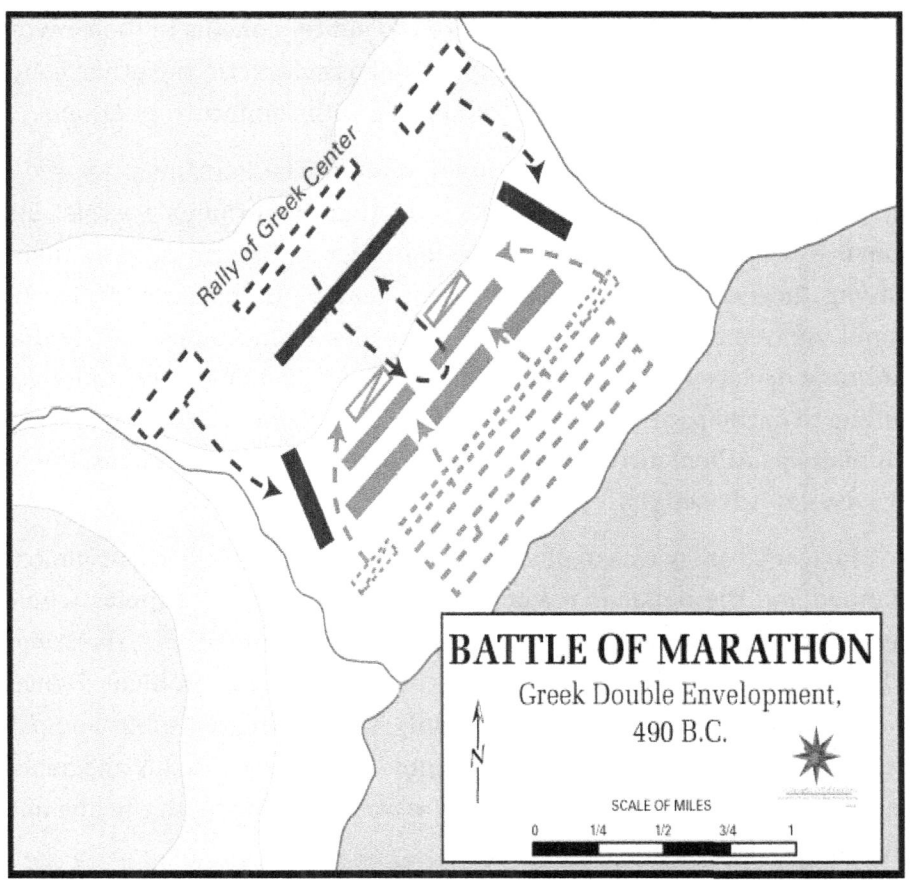

BATTLE OF MARATHON

Greek Double Envelopment,
490 B.C.

N

SCALE OF MILES

0   1/4   1/2   3/4   1

The infantry on both sides engaged in full battle formation. It was only a matter of time before the battle between the two armies would begin.

The Greeks and the Persians were both waiting for the first blow to strike to initiate the battle. Tensions were starting to escalate on both sides. Datis, commanding the Persian army, was determined to inflict a heavy penalty on the entire city of Athens and its people.

King Darius had ordered his generals to teach the Greeks a lesson not to interfere in the vast Persian Empire affairs. Their thirst for vengeance was still alive. King Darius and his mighty army only had one goal, which was to punish the Athenians who dared to aid the Ionians in their revolt against the empire and kill the Persian ambassadors. On the other hand, the Greeks wanted to get rid of Persian rule with support from Athens.

The build-up for the war was in full motion. The Persians prepared a large army and departed to Greece on their ginormous vessels and convoys. This time they were not going to let any storm destroy them. Among the Persians, the former Greek general Hippias could also be found. He was the man who had been expelled from Athens – a city that had now declared itself as a democracy. The Athenians were no longer willing to participate in what they thought of as Persian's evil oppression. Hippias was Athenian, but he had taken refugee with the Persians. It was he who had advised Datis to land their army at Marathon.

The war strategy was in place. It was set in motion. If the clash went as planned and the Persians managed to dominate Greece, Hippias would become the region's ruler. Because of his lineage to the Greeks, there was a looming suspicion that his alliance could change any moment. Hence, Datis made him swore that Hippias would have to square legions and pay tribute to the Persian Empire. If he wanted to demonstrate his allegiance and rule Athens, he had to attest that he was indeed loyal to the one and only King Darius.

The Athenian threat presented a challenge to King Darius. To secure the western frontier of the Persian empire, he trusted the former Greek general, Hippias, to be an advisor to Persian commander Datis to lead the Persians to the beaches of Marathon. The Persian troops were drawn from the vast areas of the enormous Persian Empire. The area the troops set up themselves was located next to the city of Marathon.

The Greeks, on the other hand, were getting ready as well. They were small compared to the Persians, with far fewer war resources. Grasping that the Persians were getting closer and closer by the minute, the Athenians had no other option than to ask for help. They sent on-foot messengers — the envoy they trusted and was handpicked to make the journey to Sparta. There was no way the Greeks would stand a chance against the magnificent army of Persia. They had to ask for the help of the Spartans.

Once the Greek envoy made his way over to Sparta, they witnessed an atmosphere of festival happening there. They could see the people of Sparta celebrating and wearing flowing rich mahogany robes. The Greeks, upon their arrival, made the Spartans aware of the imminent menace and threat the Persian army was about to cause them. The Spartans, however, did not comply. They sent the emissaries back by saying that they were celebrating Carnea and therefore could only send reinforcements once their ten-day feast came to an end.

For the Persian militia, this conflict was nothing more than a minor hindrance on their path to greater glory. In their eyes, the Athenians mounted to nothing in front of their might and power. Persians had the courage, excess of power, and resources, but their highly insolent nature was alarming. Hitherto for the Greeks, the stakes were very high. Their autonomy, their democracy, everything they stood for were on the line.

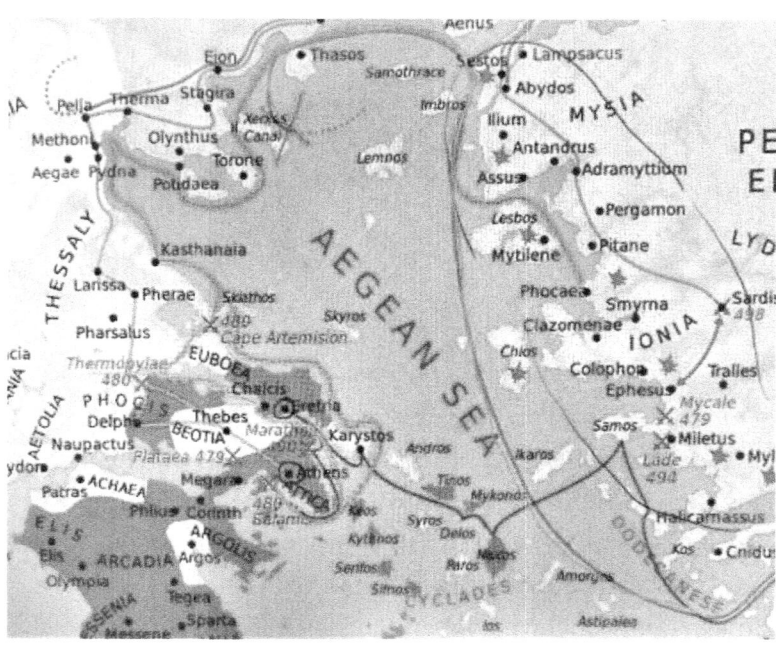

Once Datis' fleet made their touchdown on the long stretched-out beach of Marathon, the waiting game began. The Greek army, led by General Miltiades, was marching on their way. General Miltiades was a man of great valor and charisma. He was aware that the city's defense was weak. If they wanted to stand a chance against the Persians, they would have to travel onward. No one in the land dared to go against him.

The Athenians, equipped with armor and weapons, started their course to the beach of Marathon. There were just about ten thousand Greeks headed toward the fields of Marathon, where the Persian army had already settled in. As soon as the Greeks reached the top of the nearby hills, they saw the Persians' massive army. Miltiades watched his army's motion and attentively studied his troops. He professed that it would be grim to infiltrate an army of more than fifty thousand men. If he wanted the Persians to be, alarmed and frightened, they had to think of something different. Their grim chances had to be lightened. Miltiades had to evoke the gusts of courage within his men. The Greeks wanted to halt the army of the Persians. If the Persians entered the gates of their city, there would be nothing less than blood and gore.

The Greek general then thought of another plan. He decided to tactically position his troops on the top of a hill. From up there, they could see the entire convoy of the Persians. Their eyes could now spot the enormous Persian army with no less than fifty thousand entities in the flesh. The Persians had come fully prepared. They were not looking to repeat their own mistakes. King Darius' stern word was a warning to all his men.

"Make a bloody lesson out of these men of Athens." King Darius sent the message to Datis, but the battle had to wait.

Even so, with the men all up in arms, the clash took a long time to happen, for despite having fewer men, the Greeks were not a laidback foe.

The Greeks had settled at the very top of the hill, and their defensive position at the top favored them. However, the Greeks were only looking to hold the days of war until they sought after reinforcements would join them. As things stood, they were still expecting the underpinnings of help from Sparta. The Persians, who were now exposed to the Greeks' eyes, still believed that there was a looming cloud of re-emergence in the offing with Hippias. In the depths of his hearts, Hippias still believed that his troops, who were loyal to the tyrant, would split the Athenian army into two. He knew that seeing him there in flesh would arouse their spirits of allegiance and lineage.

After days and days of waiting, there were no Spartans, nor were there any men of General Hippias. As far as their eyes could see, no men from Sparta made their way to the hill where the Greeks had now set ground. On the other hand, Hippias was face to face with the truth. The trust he had in his men, the trust he was so sure would bring them to his side, had now been broken. The Persians and the Greeks were standing there with no other support.

As things stood now, there was just the approaching fear of battle that hung in front of the faces of the two armies. For neither the Spartans appeared, nor did those who are loyal to the Greek general Hippias.

Datis decided that the time had finally come when they had to fight. It was their king's destiny. He had to take back the power that was rightfully his, even if it meant destroying the Athenians. The battle could wait no more, and after waiting for a few more days, the Persians decided to act. Datis gave his army of men the command that they had waited on for days.

"Go fight this battle with courage that you are known for, go protect your honor, go slay the men who dare to disrespect your one true king, Darius." Datis' strong voice reached the hearts of the men who stood in front of him. He was aware that Persia's men would lay down their lives to protect the honor of their king.

For them, it was a matter of now or never. The Persians had a large army. Even if they divided themselves in half, there would be more men on their side. Datis knew that was the only thing working in their favor. He looked over at the men, who stood at the hill and decided to split their army. He would fragment them all, with more than twenty thousand units on one side and thirty thousand on the other.

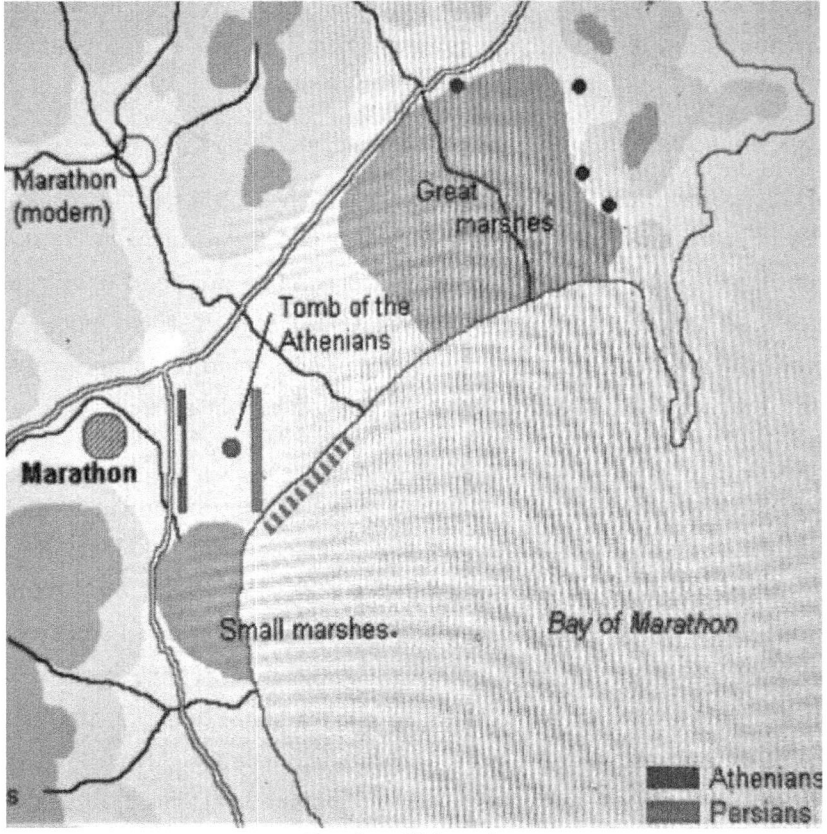

Battle of Marathon

The Persian commander, Datis, wanted a quick victory. He was proud of the army he had created, full of valiant men, always ready for war. If the Persians wanted to claim victory over Athenians, it was the right time. Oh, how much he wanted to roast them alive. Datis' strategy was to move fast for a quick victory over the Athenians.

Under the veil of darkness, when all men went to rest after a day of extensive training and the night torch was put out, Datis made his way to Artaphernes, his nephew, and spoke. "I have a plan." Datis did not have to elaborate as his loyal men could understand perfectly what he meant. He was a man of discipline, possessing a sharp mind. He did not want to fail King Darius and the trust he had placed in him.

"Yes, my leader," he said as she stood before him.

Artaphernes knew this was his cue to act. He would now lay down the details of his plan. Datis wanted to deploy his men on every nook and cranny. He wanted to sail with half of his men in the dead of the night, discreetly. The other half of the men would stay in the trenches. He grinned wickedly as he laid out the entire plan in front of Artaphernes. He wanted to carry out the plan quickly and steer his army men toward victory.

This time, they were not going to leave any stone unturned. Datis instructed his faithful general, Artaphernes, to stay at Marathon. He planned to leave behind more than thirty thousand troops with just one mission: to hold the Greek army men. On the other hand, the twenty thousand men who remained with him would be traveling by sea. They were assigned the duty to go directly to Athens and attack them from behind. The Persian army was aware that the gates of Athens were not guarded. Every Greek army man was out on the battlefield, fighting the war.

Through the night, before the sunrise, the Persians loaded their armada with horses, weapons, and other resources and left for Athens. If the Persian army's predictions were correct, Athens' city would be unguarded, and they could easily conquer the city. Datis was confident of his war plan.

The Greeks, residing in Athens, also had a defensive plan. They were not going to let the Persians ride over them so easily. The Greeks were a proud nation and couldn't tolerate being taken by any other state. They were determined to fight back.

The city of Athens didn't have the required artillery. However, the Athenians were instilled with the belief that they would fight and protect their homeland rather than be captured by Persians. The Persian army had weapons and ammunition that could instill fears into the hearts of the Greeks. Even if the Persian army was split in half, they were still a formidable force.

General Miltiades stood firm on his ground. Climbed on Marathon's mountains, the General and his ten subordinates had a clear view of the Persian army. The General could clearly see every movement and action of the Persian army. He kept a close lookout on their artilleries and formations. He noticed a gap in their strength. The Persians were without horses. Realizing that the Persians did not have their cavalry, he formulated his war strategy to take advantage of this weakness in his enemy.

Miltiades realized that there was a window of opportunity for his army. If they waited for the Persians to make the first move, they could be killed as they were outnumbered. But, if they were to take the plunge and attack now, the Greeks could take advantage of the fact that Persians did not have mounted troops with them.

Miltiades raised his sword, ready to strike, and prepared his army to commence the battle. In the eyes of his army men, this was a big risk he was taking. At any rate, the Greeks were not going to give up so easily. If victory was in their fate, this was the only way he reckoned was possible.

The Persian army was preparing for an attack. They could see them preparing for the battle. Artaphernes, looking at the unfolding events in front of him, gave his army the command to get ready.

It was just a matter of time when both armies would face each other on the battlefield. The Greek General decided to give up his strong defensive position and launch an attack. He guided his men to form a straight line of defense instead of their usual rectangular formation. He abandoned the customary, widely trusted traditional phalanx formation, and deployed his troops along the broadest possible front. His purpose was to create a thin formation in the center for the prime reason that the Persians, given their number of men, were still far greater than Greeks, and the Greeks did not match their depth. General Miltiades predicted that the Persians could corner them on both sides and surround the Greek army in just a matter of short time.

The field at the battle of Marathon was full of danger. "They'll tear us apart and shred us into pieces," feared Miltiades.

The Greek General thinned his center formation. He handpicked feeble men to stand in the front of the line. One after another, he aligned the best troops at the border. His plan was to beat the enemy's flank with his lateral troops and then help those who were fighting at the center. It was an innovative plan, yet extremely risky. The path ahead was full of thorns.

The Greek army had to face another obstacle – Persian archers, who were famous for hitting on target from a far off distance. The Greek General, aware of the imminent danger that the Persian archers presented, thought of a way out. It was an innovative idea, but it had its risk. The Greek Phalluses moved quite slowly in order to keep the formation aligned. Then once they were not too far away from the Persians, they did the unthinkable. The Greek General ordered the Greek army men to run the final hundred meters. It was a strategy to cross the death zone as fast as humanly possible.

Patient and confident, the Greeks waited for the official command, and as soon as it came, they ran as fast as they could. The Persians, however, were caught unaware of seeing the Greeks running toward them. It was something they had never thought of. It was not normal at all to see an army unit sprinting toward them.

Miltiades' idea of running their way toward the Persian army was fruitful. The Persians could not decipher what would happen next and became defensive in their formation.

The two troops were now face to face, and the bloodbath began to unfold. The ground was hard, and the one-on-one clash that unfurled next was intense.

In the beginning, the Greeks were able to fight the battle well. The Persians were constantly finding a weak spot where they could strike the Athenians. They only had one plan to show no mercy to any man who came in front of them.

The fight was steering away in another direction. Due to a large number of Persian soldiers, the center formation of the Greek army started to give in. Damage and destruction by the Persians were devastating. Artraphernes could taste victory, which was inevitable. Realizing that they were about to win, Artaphernes, the Persian General, commanded his army to push even further and strengthen the attack at the center.

However, the battle of Marathon was far from over. If the Persians wanted to win, they had to eliminate the soldiers that were carefully deployed at the edges of the formation. The wounded Greeks were still fighting. The troops that were handpicked by Miltiades fought at the flanks and managed to weaken the Persian position. They moved toward the center. The picture of the battle dramatically changed. The Persians looked vulnerable, their men were exposed, and as the tides turned, the Persian troops were now being attacked from three different directions. Panic began to spread among the Persians as they suffered heavy losses. The Greeks' victory seemed inevitable. The Persians began to withdraw and move their troops toward their ships.

On the other hand, the Persian armada, which was heading toward Athens, still had to be taken into account. So despite having been weighed down by the battle, the Greeks quickly went back home to safeguard their city. They had to inform the Athenians to stand their ground.

Commander Datis, realizing that the quick victory would be nearly impossible, ordered the Persian ships to turn back and head home. When the fleet returned, they realized the gravity of this loss.

Everything was black in the land that once danced in the pleasure of conquest. The battle had been lost. What started with anger, chaos, and violence had ended in defeat for the Persian Empire. The fresh veil of darkness that set in the empire would not dissipate any time soon. It was just a matter of time when the Mighty King was going to learn about the defeat.

No ear would be spared of the news. Tremors of the loss were felt through the entire city. As the men came to view, it was obvious what the result was. Every eye in the land watched the beaten and crushed army. As soon as the distraught men started to enter through the gates of the city, just one look was enough to narrate the entire story of what had happened. More than six thousand of King Darius' men had died trying to save the honor of their king. More than six thousand Persian homes were left without a male heir. The whole city felt the loss of those that succumbed to dirt.

Even the ones who were fortunate enough to return and step from the shadows of Marathon were not without their own teething troubles. The infantry, archers, cavalry, all the abundant supplies, the kinsmen, the fauna, all that went to Marathon was now coming back wrecked. Most of the soldiers were in pain, covered with wounds and grievances. Men who held high ranks in the army were carried up in arms to be given a proper entombment.

King Darius learned about the aftermath of the war when his loyal servants and his trusted men came back to him. The king was expecting good news. He was expecting Datis and Artrapherne, his hand-picked noblemen, to give him the news of triumph - the news he was waiting to hear for months.

But the news that awaited him was of loss. Every man who called this land home had learned of what happened at the battle. King Darius felt wronged. He was assailed by the one horrifying news he had never hoped to hear. The same robe, which he once wrapped in all its glory, the crown on his head that communicated his numerous victories, the throne that was embellished with charms was starting to feel humiliating to the king.

"How... how... how did this happen?" He roared in anger. It was the only question the king could ask his men. How could any of this happen? None of this was foreseen. The sudden uprush of emotions from him was anticipated. Thus, despite his fury, there was no answer that could calm the king's heart.

He saw this renewed face of the Greeks as a challenge to his greatness. He was burning in feelings of jealousy. The Greeks were against everything King Darius wanted. But one sole loss did not mean King Darius would stop his conquest. After this unforeseen defeat at Marathon,

Darius did not want to give up on his dream to conquer Greece. There was still a lot left to achieve in his quest for absolute rule in this land. If the Greeks had thought this would quiet him, they were wrong. King Darius was most certainly not a ruler who would feel intimidated by his opponents.

All his life, he had fought hard for recognition, for respect. Just one defeat was not going to overturn it all. Never in a million moon would he let that happen. He wanted to crush all his competition to become the greatest Persian Emperor of all time, but the Greeks had something else in their mind. The next decision that the Great King was about to take would only be driven by ambition, jealousy, hatred, and revenge.

"What was King Darius going to do?" was the one question plastered inside everyone's mind. The same man who ordered the seizure of the Greek land when he learned of the rebellion would surely think of something a lot harsher. His mind was caught with the reality that his men came back not only empty-handed but after being humiliated by an undermanned army of his foes.

That night, after his men gave him the news of the defeat, the king stood in his veranda, without any direction of what to do next. He marched on the granite floor back and forth. The sound of his footsteps could communicate his uneasiness and anxiety. His next move had to be strategic, or he could risk losing the empire he worked so hard for.

A voice behind him was stepped out in hopes of comforting him, "My king, why do you worry?" It was Artystone, his wife. She placed her gentle hands on his shoulder for comfort.

"Because I fear my men feel defeated," King Darius wanted to be remembered as the greatest Emperor in all of the lands, yet the fear of the unknown was slowly taking over his mind.

"They are all brave men serving a Great King. There will always be more battles to win, Darius," she consoled, looking at the view of splendid Persepolis under the moonlight.

King Darius' eyes followed her gaze, and he looked out at the land that stretched in front of his eyes, "I shall kill them all, I shall finish them." He was almost fuming with anger.

"In due time, my king, you will have your revenge." Her last parting words stayed with him. She was right. He was not going to let this one setback defeat him and his spirits. He was going to keep the promise he had made — the promise to bring honor to the land of his people. Ahura Mazda had blessed him with this power. It was his destiny to rule. He could not let it bring him down.

The only answer to all of this was uprise was another battle. King Darius had won so many wars. He had expanded his regime to countless cities, but things this time were different.

Without wasting any more precious seconds of his days, he ordered his military commanders to enter his throne room, and they all followed through. These were the few lucky men who were spared by death itself. One by one, all of them entered his chamber, awaiting the commands that were headed for their way. All the men stood close to one another and looked at the king, who had called them here. They all knew this was a matter of grave urgency.

Once everyone had settled, the king began to speak. "The culprits, who dare challenge me, need to be brought to their knees," the King announced to the hall full of men. His voice was louder than they had ever heard before. "But this time, we will not send any army, any fleet in a hurry. This time we will prepare. We will train hard and then send an army that is impossible to defeat." He walked back to the throne he held so dear to him.

"Sire, if you don't mind me interrupting, what are you thinking?" A man from amidst the shadows spoke. He was in charge of the fleet of Cyprus.

"An earth-shaking conflict," King Darius proclaimed. "To avenge this loss." His face was like stone. He found the result of the war insulting to his very existence, but he would not let this end his purpose. With hope in his heart and vision for Persia in his eyes, the next few years of the Persian Empire passed in which he was a proud king who cared about his empire. He was not going to look back on this loss. This time, he was going to lead the army himself. He used the loss at Marathon as his one true driving force. With time the king gathered and prepared an even larger army to conquer and take revenge from the Greeks and expand his empire.

Chapter 13: The Legacy of Darius the Great

Persia the First Real Empire

King Darius ended up creating a victorious montage of a realm that would live on in this world for centuries. Many territories and landmasses were taken control of after the many battles King Darius and his army partook in. His every success was attributed to the mighty Ahura Mazda. His countless military conquest expanded the boundaries of Persia. The purpose he had for Persia will always be engraved in every memory that grows to learn about him. The king's vision for his empire is a classic example for kingdoms and countries to come.

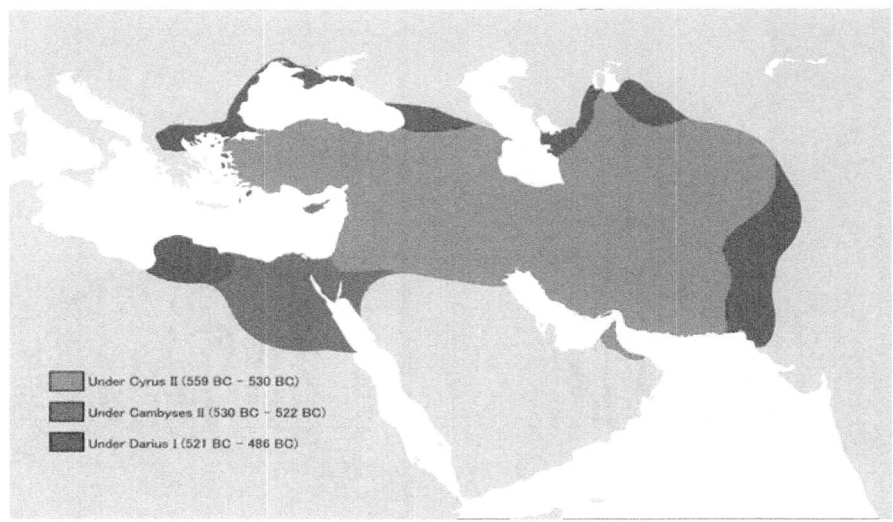

Persian Empire

It was under this Mighty King's reign that Persia established itself as the first real empire in the world. As years passed, the Persians only saw triumph in their path. For as long as he lived, he vowed to bring greatness to the land. The Empire saw a lot of ups and downs. Even with a handful of defeats that became part of his fate, he stood fast in his decree. The

Persian Empire witnessed many acquisitions, rebuttals, revolts, and accomplishments during King Darius' reign.

The Great King of Persia is credited with the honor of building an empire possessing an organizational structure, systems, and established strategy that is inked in history books. In the lands that were under Persian control, he promised to govern a realm free from any prejudice and hate, and, as long as the king lived, the lands that submitted to him thrived with peace.

Some of his many rules and strategies have managed to survive.

Inventions and Innovations

Persia's reputation now grew and grew, ranging far in the land. Tales of the king's ideas and his admirable manifestation for Persia became the talk of his Empire. As king of kings, Darius undertook impressive construction projects across the empire. More significant than his conquests, though, were the measures he took to bring great inventions to the world. The Persian Empire, under his rule, by the grace of Ahuramazda, established the most improved and advanced Empire in the world. His time in power should be attributed to some of the most renowned inventions and maintained amenities, policies, practices, institutions, and aspects of religion – all of these to date are well-known.

However, for centuries credit has been taken away from the Great King. The Persian Empire has given the modern world a lot, which the ordinary public uses today. However, for ages, so many of these advanced inventions are not often properly attributed to them. It has been a never-ending struggle for the possession of their due credit. Some of their time-less inventions include:

- First Declaration of Human Rights

- Irrigation and Refrigeration

- New-Year Celebration

- Landscaped Gardens and the Word 'Paradise'

- Birthday Celebrations, Animation, and Dessert

- Monotheism

- Elite Military Units – Immortals

- Windmills

- Air Conditioning

- Postal System

- Monetary System

- Highway – Royal Rods

- The Teaching Hospital

- Heavily Armored Cavalry

- Wine

- Guitar

Darius only saw one task ahead of him, which was to make Persia the greatest empire to ever exist, and the king succeeded in doing that. However, today, for certain, this sound common and ordinary. However, centuries ago, they were something no one had heard of. These inventions were entirely novel in their time. Even though there were gardens in other cultures, and monotheism had been suggested by the Egyptian pharaoh Akhenaten centuries before, the Persians. King Darius and his domain of trusted men were the first to develop these concepts fully.

First Declaration of Human Rights

In 539 B.C., Cyrus the Great, after conquering the city of Babylon, did something that was unimaginable at that time. The king who ruled before Darius freed all the slaves. He made them return to their original homes. This clay tablet dates back to the reign of that King, Cyrus the Great. The text claims that Cyrus restored temples in the neighboring cities and returned deported people to their homes. With reference to his just and peaceful rule, this cylinder has been referred to as an early charter of human rights.

The clay tablet is known as *The Cyrus Cylinder*. It is inscribed with a cuneiform script issued by Cyrus. It is an official document that tells of Cyrus the Great's conquest of the various regions which made up the Achaemenid Empire and how they had embraced his rule. He then speaks of how he elevated the people's lives through the rights and liberties granted them. The cylinder shows Cyrus saying, "The gods who dwelt there, I returned to their home and let them move into an eternal dwelling. All the people I collected and brought them back to their homes."

For centuries, the tablet was never given due recognition, but now for the last few decades, it is recognized as the first declaration of human rights in the world. The Achaemenid Empire granted its citizens freedom of religious thought and practices as well as many other liberties denied those of other cultures, including almost equal rights for women.

Irrigation and Refrigeration

The concepts of irrigation and refrigeration are also often attributed to Cyrus the Great. These systems might have generated in his reign, but they were not used until King Darius came to power. These innovations were actually invented by earlier Persian innovators and attested during the time of the Assyrian king Sargon II, who ruled way before King Darius and even Cyrus.

The process of underground tunnel systems that brings infiltrated groundwater was also invented in the Great King's tenure. It was popularly referred to as *the qanat system.* It worked when a sloping channel was dug into the earth with vertical shafts at intervals drawing water up from underground aquifers and served to irrigate otherwise arid lands and turned them into lush landscapes.

The *qanat* system worked in order to moisten the farmlands. It watered farm fields and allowed for the cultivation of elaborate gardens.

The *yakhchal* was a domed refrigeration unit made of clay used to store ice. It was also utilized to keep food cold.

Landscaped Gardens and the Word 'Paradise'

Darius also finished previously incomplete construction projects of Cyrus in the Empire. Under Darius' rule, the *qanat* enabled the cultivation of landscaped gardens, which became a regular feature of Persian architectural design. Even Cyrus was said to have spent as much time in his gardens as possible. The king would stay in the garden before attending to the business of running his empire. This practice was adopted by King Darius as well.

The traditional style of Persian garden design known as Paradise. The Paradise garden, has influenced the design of gardens from India, to Europe and America.

Birthday Celebrations, Animation, Wine and Dessert

As so often in its unfortunate history, The Persians were not given their share when it came to celebrations. The Persians were the first to develop the practice of lavish celebrations of one's birthday as well as the art of animation for entertainment and the custom of having dessert after a big meal. The Persians would celebrate the day when one was born. However, not every man or woman was to be celebrated.

Birthday celebrations honored only the monarch's birth, but, with time, gradually, the nature of celebrations spread to members of the nobility and then after the king's death onto the lower classes.

Monotheism

When it came to religion, it is not a secret that Darius was an adherent of Zoroastrianism and a firm believer of Ahura Mazda. Slowly, the whole of Persian took under the wing of Zoroastrianism. Most men held the same belief that there was only one supreme being, Ahura Mazda. It was all because of King Darius and his wife, Queen Atusa, that the religion spread.

Soon the purpose of one's life was to follow the will of the benevolent God through the principles of Good Thoughts, Good Words, and Good Deeds. Zoroastrianism also was the first faith to fully develop the concepts of heaven, hell, and purgatory. Not only resuming bureaucracy, but Darius also improved the military prowess. Even when it came to military personnel and their ranks of the immortal Persian guards, they were given their ranks according to who the king trusted the most and how they passed away. The famous glazed bricks friezes found in the Apadana *(Darius the Great's palace)* in Susa showed ranks of those who died and were now deemed *immortal*. There were more than 10,000 royal guards in the Persian regime. If any guard passed away, they were replaced straight away, thus explaining their name of immortals. However, not everyone could become immortal. You had to be special. You had to have the blood of those who Darius confide in. Only Persian and Median nobles could become immortals.

Windmills and Air Conditioning

The standard of living in Persia rose under King Darius' rule. The Persians used the windmills, although it is not clear if the Persians truly did invent the windmills, for the first recorded mention of the devices were earlier. However, after King Darius came to power, windmills were famously used in pumping water and grinding grain. They were made of reeds woven together into paddles, which were then fixed to a central axis.

The concept was almost certainly suggested by the use of the sail on ships. However, the Persians were already making use of wind on land through the ventilation system known as the windcatcher, which looked like a tower that was responsible for generating wind. It worked as a structure was attached to the top of a building, which helped draw cool air down, pushing warmer air up and out.

First Postal System

Darius' reforms improved the strength of the Empire. He gave importance to messengers and how efficiently these messages were conveyed. King Daris knew how vital these messages were when the Empire was on the brink of war.

If an essential message reached the king and his army personnel a minute later, it could cause serious consequences. This is why the king gave extra attention to the postal system. In his regime, the concept of the highway was also developed. King Darius instituted the Persian network of roads for improving travel speed and contact between his capital cities *(Babylon, Ecbatana, Persepolis, and Susa.)* The highways were then used to send messages between these cities as well as others, thus creating the postal system.

Monetary System

During Darius' reign, he established the world's first bimetallic monetary system and created a standard structure for tax collection from empire's vast states and territories.

Gold Daric Minted at Sardis

Darius statue on the top of Berlin Central Post office building in recognition of Darius the Great invention of the first Postal System in the world

First Highway – Royal Roads

The Royal Road was an ancient highway built by the order of Darius in the 5th century B.C.E. Persians built the road to facilitate rapid communication throughout their very vast empire from Susa to Ecbatana, Babylon, and Sardis. Mounted courier travel 1,677 miles (2,699 km) from

Susa to Sardis in nine days, the journey took over two hundred days on foot.

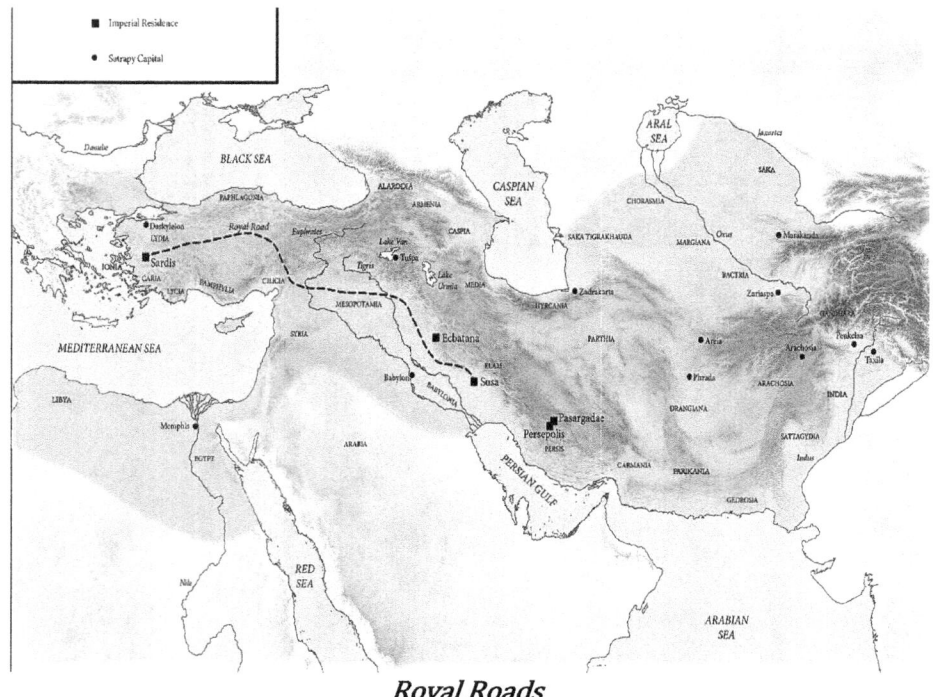

Royal Roads

Darius Canal - The 1st Suez Canal

The modern-day Suez Canal in Egypt opened in 1869, connecting the Mediterranean Sea to the Red Sea. It offered a shorter shipping route between the Atlantic and Indian Oceans via the Mediterranean and the Red Sea.

The Suez Canal of today is an ancient concept. A fully functional canal was engineered and completed by King Darius of Persia in 500 B.C.

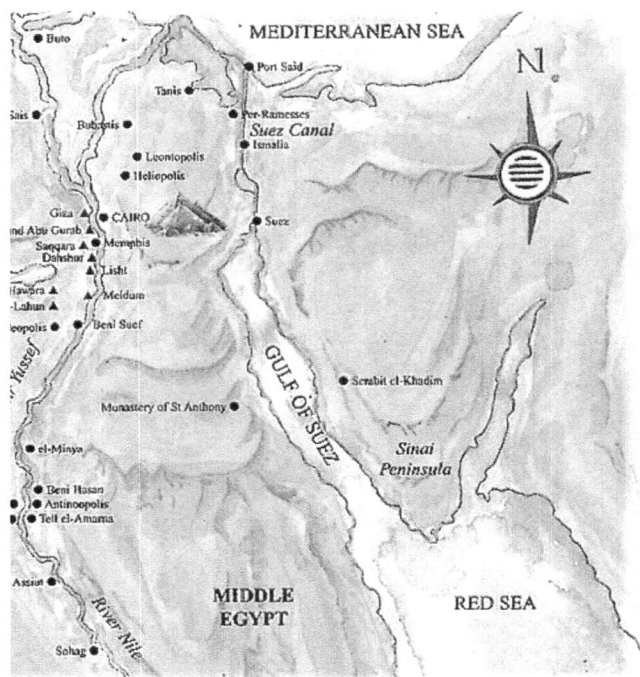

Darius created five monuments in Egypt and named Darius the Great's Suez Inscriptions to document his achievements. The monuments contained texts written in Old Persian, Egyptian, Babylonian, and Elamite announcing the opening of a canal between the Nile and the Bitter Lakes. The primary purpose of the canal was the creation of a shipping route between Egypt and Persia. The inscriptions read:

"King Darius says: I am a Persian, setting out from Persia. I conquered Egypt. I ordered to dig this canal from the river that is called the Nile and flows in Egypt to the sea that begins in Persia. Therefore, when this canal had been dug as I had ordered, ships went from Egypt through this canal to Persia, as I had intended."

STÈLE DE CHALOUF.

Débris du texte en caractères cunéiformes.

Darius the Great's Suez Inscriptions
Louvre Museum – Paris

King Darius as the Pheroah of Egypt at the Temple of Hibis

Elite Force - Immortals

The Persians were the first to develop the concept of an elite force called Immortals in the ancient world. There were 10,000 royal guards, any dead being replaced straight away, explaining their name of Immortals. Only Persian and Median nobles were eligible to join this elite force. They were selected at an early age and sent to special training camps, and would go through an elaborate, rigorous, and comprehensive education and military training. They were armed with bows, shields, and lances. Each unit was commanded by an officer named Chyliarchs. According to the historian Pierre Briant, who rejected the general idea from the Greek historians, reports that despite their rich and colorful uniforms, these soldiers were neither a parade unit nor some royal guard units but an elite fighting force that was engaged in most of the Persian wars.

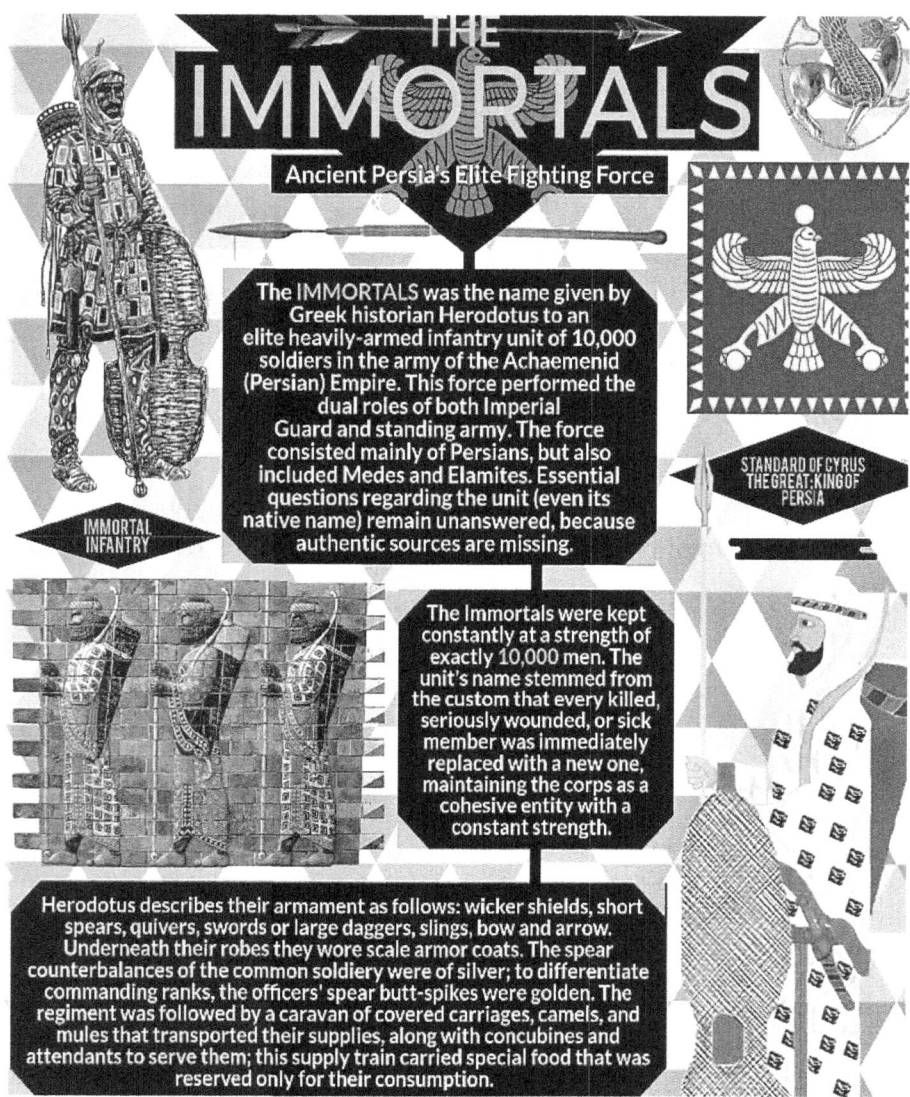

THE IMMORTALS

Ancient Persia's Elite Fighting Force

The IMMORTALS was the name given by Greek historian Herodotus to an elite heavily-armed infantry unit of 10,000 soldiers in the army of the Achaemenid (Persian) Empire. This force performed the dual roles of both Imperial Guard and standing army. The force consisted mainly of Persians, but also included Medes and Elamites. Essential questions regarding the unit (even its native name) remain unanswered, because authentic sources are missing.

IMMORTAL INFANTRY

STANDARD OF CYRUS THE GREAT: KING OF PERSIA

The Immortals were kept constantly at a strength of exactly 10,000 men. The unit's name stemmed from the custom that every killed, seriously wounded, or sick member was immediately replaced with a new one, maintaining the corps as a cohesive entity with a constant strength.

Herodotus describes their armament as follows: wicker shields, short spears, quivers, swords or large daggers, slings, bow and arrow. Underneath their robes they wore scale armor coats. The spear counterbalances of the common soldiery were of silver; to differentiate commanding ranks, the officers' spear butt-spikes were golden. The regiment was followed by a caravan of covered carriages, camels, and mules that transported their supplies, along with concubines and attendants to serve them; this supply train carried special food that was reserved only for their consumption.

Perspolis Persia

Wine

Wine is a fermented drink from grapes. Wine originated in 6,000-3,000 BC in Persia.

Detail of a relief on the eastern stairs of the Apadana Palace, Persepolis, depicting Armenian ambassadors, bringing the best wines to the Persian Emperor.

Epilog

Prayer, ritual, and sacrifice – that's all it took for King Darius to become the King of Persia. The Mighty King's rise to power moved from stories, myths, and folklore and is told around the world. Whether it's the staged co-up or the Persian's unforeseen loss at Marathon, his regime saw it all.

Darius, to whom Persia owes much, gave the territory its direction and set it in its way. Darius' reign was one of the most significant occurrences in the history of the Persian Empire. The world knows what happened to Cyrus the Great, yet more than half of the world is oblivious to what Darius achieved. The resultant debacle reveals all the marvelous qualities of King Darius' mind. The Persians, under the Great King, went on to do greater things. And, to date, they are known to be one of the most visionary and talented societies that existed in the past. If it wasn't for them and their many inventions, the modern world would not be as advanced as it is now.

His rise to become the king of the Persian Empire was because of a carefully planned coup, but soon coups became part of his destiny. Darius wanted to become the king because he deemed no other man worthy of this status. He wanted to claim the throne, and when he did, he was met with resilience. Nothing came easy to the king. Darius had inherited a loosely organized kingdom, and he spent his first three years quelling uprisings. As such, before his death, he made sure to unite and assimilate the ones who inhabited the land of Persia. And when King Darius died, there were no rebellions comparable to those who were born when he settled onto the throne.

The king's set of beliefs stayed with him until his very last day. Not once did the king become weak. Even when the king laid on his death bed, suffering from severe illness, he wanted his last words to be original and sincere:

"My body is strong. As a fighter of battles, I am a good fighter of battles. [...] I am skilled both in hands and in feet. A horseman, I am a good horseman. A bowman, I am a good bowman, both on foot and on horseback. A spearman, I am a good spearman, both on foot and on horseback. These skills that Ahuramazda set down upon me..."

To date, this is how the great King Darius wanted to be remembered. At the end of the Mighty King's long and prosperous life, as he continued to consolidate and expand his conquests, came a day when all of it had to be laid to rest with him. When the king passed away in October 486 B.C.E, his body had to be prepared for the afterlife. The body of the king of kings was balmed, placed in a coffin, and transported to Naqsh-e Rustam, where his tomb had been prepared a long time ago. After his death, the throne was inherited by Xerxes, his son from his marriage with Atusa, daughter of Cyrus the Great.

Naqsh-e Rustam is located about five kilometers to the northwest of Persepolis, the capital city of the Persian Empire. It is a spectacular ancient site containing the tombs of four great Persian kings, namely Darius The Great, Xerxes, Artaxerxes, and Darius II. This site stands as the last memory of a vast, powerful empire that ruled over 48% of the ancient world. This is further echoed in the inscription from Darius' tomb from Naqsh-e Rustam: Darius, the king, proclaims: **By the favor of Ahuramazda these are the countries which I seized outside Persia; I ruled over them; they bore me tribute; what was said to them by me, that they did; my law that held them (firm); Media, Elam, Parthia, Areia, Bactria, Sogdiana, Chorasmia, Drangiana, Arachosia, Sattagydia, Gandara, India, Saca who drink hauma, Saca with pointed hats Babylonia, Assyria, Arabia, Egypt, Armenia, Cappadocia, Sardis, Ionia, Scythians who are across the sea, Thrace, petasos-wearing Ionians, Libya, Nubia, Maka, Caria.**

Darius' Tomb at Naqsh-e-Rustam, Persia

Darius' Tomb at Naqsh-e-Rustam, Persia

Darius The Great

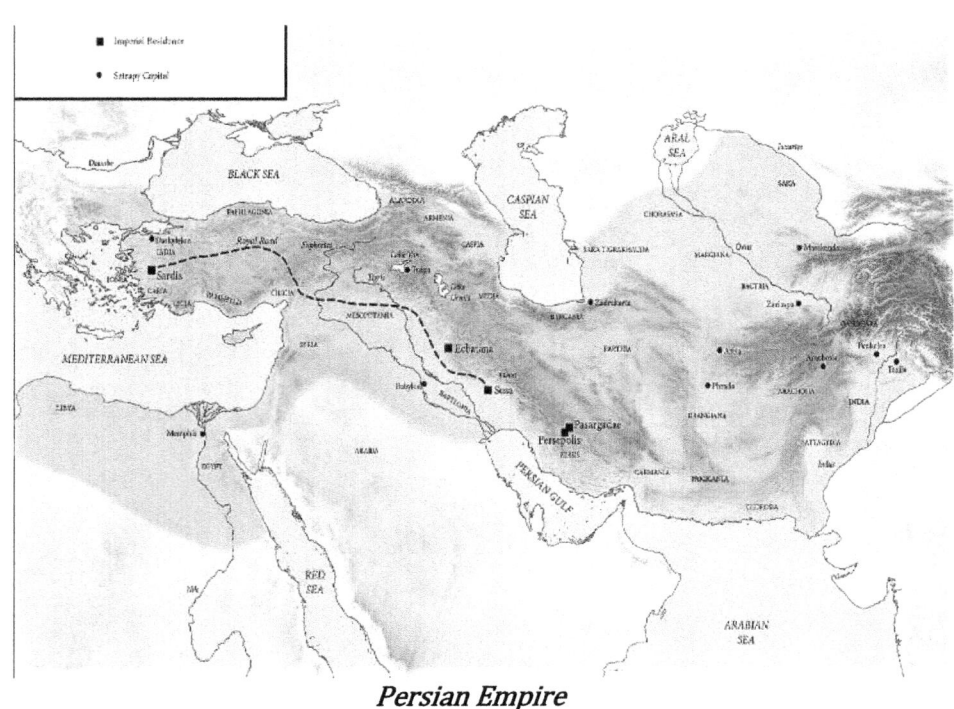

Persian Empire

www.cyrusthemovie.com

About the Movie

Cyrus Production Company, Inc. is in pre-production of the motion picture **Cyrus: The Rise of Empire**. A historical epic movie based on this book.

The Story

Twenty-five hundred years ago, Cyrus the Great, a leader of wisdom and virtue and enduring influence, created the Persian Empire, conquered Babylon, freed the Jews from captivity, formulated mankind's first human rights charter, ruled over those he conquered with respect and benevolence, and changed the course of world history. A fast-paced drama of the life of Cyrus the Great that begins when he is kidnapped at birth because of prophecy and left to die in the wilderness. The beginnings of a heroic warrior destined to become the founder of an empire that would stretch from Europe and Egypt to Middle East and India. In the tradition of films like Braveheart, Gladiator, Ben-Hur, and the Ten Commandments, Cyrus the Great is an epic retelling of one of the most extraordinary men who ever lived.

We believe more people should be aware of his story and how he changed world history. And more importantly, how his message of human rights, diversity, freedom of Religion, and tolerance is still valid today.

Logline

CYRUS: RISE OF EMPIRE is an epic historical drama about Cyrus The Great, prophesized by birth to change the world, a prince raised in secret by a family of shepherds, who must discover who he is and fulfill his destiny to be a liberator of slaves, a protector, and servant to all humanity, and the ruler of the largest empire in the history of the world.

Epic Action Film

The Epic Action film isn't just making a comeback... **it's back.** Hollywood is once again obsessed with the ancient world and is hungry to consume movies and tv shows that can take them back in time to the lost world. While in the 70's and 80's, production companies had to build out massive sets that cost thousands to create an Epic film, today, with new innovative technologies, it is more affordable than ever to produce a blockbuster.

Our Movie has a Message

Besides bringing to life the legacy of one of the most extraordinary individuals to ever live, *Cyrus The Great* has a strong theme that the world needs to hear. While *Cyrus* was building one of the largest empires the world had ever seen, he was doing it in such a way that was humane and harmonious. He ruled and conquered to unite the world under his benevolent and strategic leadership. He created the first Human Rights Charter, with freedom of religion, speech, customs, and employment. *Cyrus* led with unparalleled genius and established a humanistic-based strategy and leadership style that was respected and observed by all. If *Cyrus* was able to govern one of the largest empires to ever exist through harmony... **what can we learn from his leadership and philosophy and apply to today's conflicts in the world?**

Our Team

Alan J. Bailey
President & Executive
— Producer —

Dr. Alex Parsinia
Producer & Co-Writer

Adam Krentzman
Executive Producer

Thane Swigart
Screen Writer

ALAN J. BAILEY

President of
Cyrus the Great Production Company
Executive Producer

Professor Alan Baily is the founder, CEO and CFO of Dynamic Media Group, Inc. based in Century City, California, which is a new media entertainment company with three operating divisions: Dynamic Media Network, the producer and distributor of Dynamic Media Network, the producer and distributor of high definition original TV content; Dynamic Media Music, the producer and distributor of original music content; and Dynamic Media Pictures, an independent motion picture and television production, finance and global distribution enterprise.

Previously, Alan was a Senior Financial Executive with Paramount Pictures for 35 years, including being its Senior Vice President and Treasurer. In this capacity he was responsible for Paramount's global financial management, including working and closing deals with investors seeking to invest in Paramount's motion picture etc. Currently, Alan acts as a "virtual" CFO to a number of publicly traded companies primarily engaged in aspects of the motion picture and television industry, and he is fully familiar with SEC reporting (10K's and 10Q's etc.), reverse mergers and acquisition, OTC Pink Sheet alternative reporting, preparation of business plans, financial accounting and reporting, S- 1's, Regulation D (504) and Regulation A filings, business modelling and budgeting.

DR. ALEX PARSINIA

Producer / Co-Writer

Dr. Alex Parsinia is Chairman and Professor at American Premier University. Dr. Parsinia was a Professor at Pepperdine University in Malibu, California State University in Northridge, California and International American University in Los Angeles. He taught Business Strategy International Business, Organizational Leadership, Organizational Behavior and Mergers and Acquisitions. He has a Bachelor of Science Degree in Mechanical Engineering, Master of Business Administration and Ph.D. in International Business. He is a Certified Merger and Acquisition Specialist and has published books and numerous professional articles in national and international journals. Dr. Parsinia has an extensive background in senior level management,

Mergers and Acquisitions and more than fifteen years of experience in the Media, Manufacturing and Telecommunication industries. He was the Chairman and CEO of Global Gateway Media & Communications, Inc., a publicly traded company. He has been the CEO of Supertel Communications, Inc. (Telecom), JDS Services with revenues of over $500 million, Signet Paper Company, Pioneer Envelope Company, and Allied Corporate Investments.

LARRY HEDRICK

BOARD OF ADUISOR MEMBER
The Arts of Leadership and War
(Xenophon the Historian)

Xenophon's masterpiece The Education of Cyrus-- a work admired by Machiavelli for its lessons on leadership--is at last available in a new English translation for a new century. Also known as the Cyropaedia, this philosophical novel is loosely based on the accomplishments of Cyrus the Great, founder of the vast Persian Empire that later became the archrival of the Greeks in the classical age. It offers an extraordinary portrait of political ambition, talent, and their ultimate limits.

The writings of Xenophon are increasingly recognized as important works of political philosophy. In The Education of Cyrus, Xenophon confronts the vexing problem of political instability by exploring the character and behavior of the ruler. Impressive though his successes are, however, Cyrus is also examined in the larger human context, in which love, honor, greed, revenge, folly, piety, and the search for wisdom all have important parts to play.

Adam Krentzman - Executive Producer

Adam Krentzman is one of the most well-respected executives in the motion picture business. For 25 years he has been involved with packaging, producing, and arranging the financing on over 50 feature films. As a longtime agent at CAA, Krentzman knows the entertainment as a longtime agent at CAA, Mr. Krentzman knows the entertainment industry landscape. CAA is the most prominent and esteemed motion picture, television, and music agency in the history of the entertainment industry. For 20-years Mr. Krentzman served as a motion picture agent representing Hollywood's top directors, producers, and writers.

His clients included: Michael Bay, Francis Ford Coppola, Michael Mann, Antoine Fuqua, Jerry Bruckheimer, Sundance Films, and National Geographic. He was also the Chief Operating Officer of Hollywood Gang – producers of The Departed, 300 The Immortals and Se7en. Mr. Krentzman has taught and or lectured both graduate and undergraduate courses on Hollywood business practices and film financing at various universities including: Beijing Film Academy, USC, UCLA, Loyola Marymount, University of Hawaii, University of Arizona, American Film Institute, Academy of Art University, National Film School of Florence, Boston University, and Columbia College.

THANE SWIGART - SCREEN WRITER

Thane Swigart is Chief Creative Officer of Light Brigade Entertainment, based in Santa Barbara, CA, co-founded with producing partner Lowell Blank in 2010. He has a degree in Anthropology from UCLA and is a Fellow of the Royal Geographical Society. He has developed projects with directors Jean-Jacques Annaud, Andrew Davis, James Foley, Dominic Sena, Mennen Yapo, and the visionary Japanese director Ryuhei Kitamura. He lived in Beijing in 2010 to develop "Spiritual Sword" for Dragonvision International, a film based on the popular Chinese video game. In 2016 he wrote "Never Again", for producers Jenette Kahn and Adam Richman (Clint Eastwood's "Gran Torino", Colin Trevorrow's "Book of Henry"), based on the New Yorker articles by Lawrence Weschler.

His screenplay "John Frum" is currently in pre-production financed by Bloom Media and BCDF Pictures and produced by Claude dal Farra, Double Nickel Entertainment's Jenette Kahn and Adam Richman, Light Brigade Entertainment's Lowell Blank, and producer Nathan Ross ("Dallas Buyer's Club", "Wild," "Big Little Lies"). His next project is "Red Bom" a scripted series for Sky Vision and Double Nickel Entertainment.

Cannes Film Festival

We exhibited Cyrus: The Rise of Empire at Cannes Film Festival, an annual event held in Cannes, France. This is the most prestigious film festival in the world, which previews new films of all genres from all across the world. It is the most powerful location to network with producers, directors, strategic partners, co-production partners, and international distribution agents. Below are some of the pictures of this festival and our booth at the event.

CANNES FILM FESTIVAL 2018

We exhibited at Cannes Film Festival at Cannes France from May 9. 2018 to May 14. 2018. Cannes Film Festival is the most prestigious film festival in the world. It is an annual event held in Cannes, France, which previews new films of all genres from all around the world as well as it is the most powerful location to network with producers, directors, strategic partners, co-production partners and international distribution agents.

"CYRUS"
The Motion Picture

www.CyrusTheMovie.com · 310.962.0085

Alan Bailey

Armand Asante

Dr. Alex Parsinia Mania Minooy

Bill Gottlieb

Adam Krentzman

UCLA Film Festival

UCLA Film Festival

DAVOOD ROOSTAEI WITH MAYOR ERIC GARCETTI

Presentation of Cyrus the Great painting to the City of Los Angeles with Mayor Eric Garcetty and City Council members in Los Angeles City Hall on March 17,2018. This painting has been placed permanently in the City Hall, Los Angeles, California.

The Founding Fathers of the United States, especially Thomas Jefferson, John Adams and Benjamin Franklin were strongly influenced by Cyrus the Great's legacy of governance based on respect for freedom of religion, customs, language and traditions.

This painting by Davood Roostaei depicts the fact that the Founding fathers of the United States admired and consulted Cyrus' legacy of governance as described in the Cyropaedia. Thomas Jefferson recommended two books to be read by fellow members representing two opposing ideology: Xenophon's Cyropaedia and Machiavel's Prince. At the end, our Founding Fathers selected Cyrus's vision.

BEVERLY HILLS CITY WITH MAYOR JULIAN GOLD

Cyrus The Great Movie Event in Beverly Hills City Hall

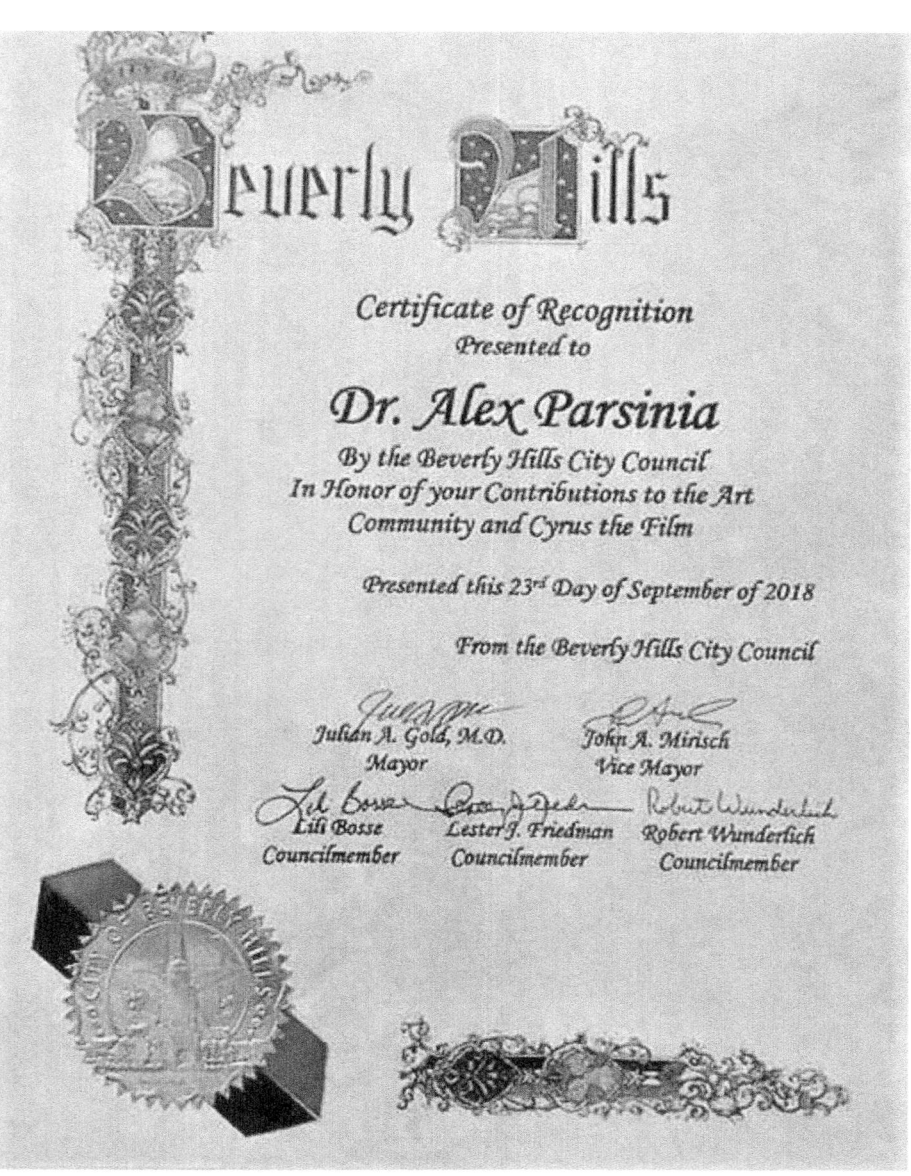

Book Published by Dr. Alex Parsinia
Cyrus: The Rise of Empire

Twenty-five hundred years ago, Cyrus the Great, a leader of wisdom and virtue and enduring influence, created the Persian Empire, conquered Babylon, freed the Jews from captivity, formulated mankind's first human rights charter, ruled over those he conquered with respect and benevolence, and changed the course of world history. The beginnings of a heroic warrior destined to become the founder of Persian empire that would stretch from Eastern Europe and Egypt to Middle East and India. Cyrus the Great is an epic retelling of one of the most extraordinary men who ever lived.

Cyrus: A Celebrated Hero

We are living in a time when we truly lack Heroes and Role Models for our children, grandchildren and generations to fol- low. Cyrus personifies that Hero with qualities that can be rec- ognized and celebrated.

His values founded on the bedrock of human rights, diversity, justice, freedom of religion, abolition of slavery and tolerance are all Core Human Values. The strong message of this book is to celebrate the recognition of these values which ultimately save humanity and promote peace and harmony globally.

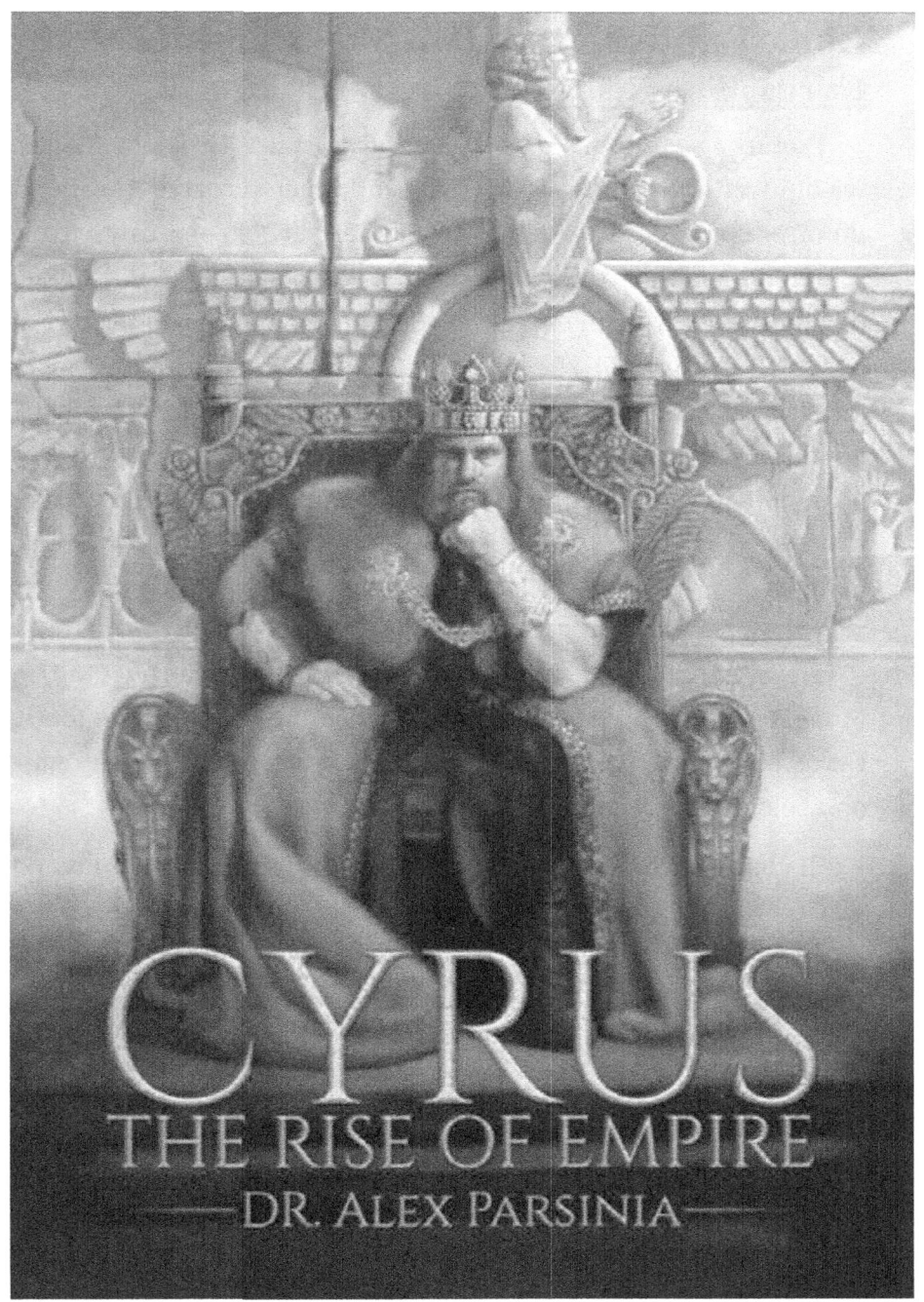

CYRUS
THE RISE OF EMPIRE

About the Author

Professor Parsinia is a prolific writer and has published books and numerous articles. He is in the process of completing two additional books related to the Achaemenid Empire - Darius Empire Builder and Xerxes Clash of Empires. He is the Producer of the Motion Picture Cyrus: The Rise of Empire. The movie is in pre-production and the story is based on this book. Dr. Parsinia is a professor of Strategy and International Business. He was a Professor at Pepperdine University and California State University. He has a Bachelor of Science Degree in Mechanical Engineering, Master of Business Administration, and Ph.D. in International Business.

About the Book

Twenty-five hundred years ago, Cyrus the Great, a leader of wisdom and virtue and enduring influence, created the Persian Empire, conquered Babylon, freed the Jews from captivity, formulated mankind's first human rights charter, ruled over those he conquered with respect and benevolence, and changed the course of world history. The beginnings of a heroic warrior destined to become the founder of Persian empire that would stretch from Eastern Europe and Egypt to Middle East and India. Cyrus the Great is an epic retelling of one of the most extraordinary men who ever lived.

We are living in a time when we truly lack Heroes and Role Models for our children, grandchildren and generations to follow. Cyrus personifies that Hero with qualities that can be recognized and celebrated. His values founded on the bedrock of human rights, diversity, justice, freedom of religion, abolition of slavery and tolerance are all Core Human Values. The strong message of this book is to celebrate the recognition of these values which ultimately save humanity and promote peace and harmony globally.

——DR. ALEX PARSINIA——

Made in the USA
Monee, IL
30 September 2021

78727002R00154